FREDERICK JAMES PRESTON

DO as I SAY,

NOT as I DO

To my friend Terry McKnight
All we need
is a little love

frederick
9/24/05

Written In Black
Publishing

www.frederickpreston.com

Published by Written In Black Publishing
P.O. Box 9303, Jacksonville, Florida 32208

Printed in the United States of America

Acknowledgements

There is no way I'm going to get myself in trouble by trying to name everyone who played a part in making this dream come true. If you know that you helped me, believe that I know it, too and I thank you more than words–or money–can say.

To the One who always has an answer for me, Jesus Christ, thank you for allowing me to believe in the talents and abilities you bestowed upon me.

Special thanks goes out to the people who let me think I'm right about everything I say, out of fear of hurting my feelings. Thanks Frederick III, Roderick, Mercedez, Porsha, Rodney, LeAndra, Mike O, Kenny, Michelle, Nicholas, and Pastor Roderick Ware–I finally wrote it down, but to this group, in particular, thanks for being down for whatever.

To every school board employee, Head Start employee, barber, or hairstylist in America who ever gave me a dime, if you didn't know it before, I appreciate it from the bottom of my heart. You gave me the encouragement, the confidence–and the money to pay the light bill so that I could focus on my dream.

Mama and Daddy, you're always the last to know because I want to surprise you the most.

Thank you Chandra Sparks Taylor, my editor, for your guidance. You know how much it meant to me that you deemed me worthy of your presence, may this book be further proof of your genius.

Thanks to the Mitchells, the Prestons, the Knights, the Ramseurs, and everyone in North Carolina who's a past or present *Defeat the Beat* affiliate, I've learned so much from you–some of it I'm afraid to put in a book.

To my big sister Vicci and the Wileys in the world, some things I cannot change. Love me for me, as I love you for you.

Many of you silently thought I would never make it this far with this project; your body language gave you away. Thanks for the motivation.

Frederick   6.10.04   2:12 A.M.

Do as I Say, Not as I Do

PROLOGUE

I hadn't been at school more than a couple of hours when the first round of gunfire and the accompanying sirens echoed throughout the neighborhood.

Confident that the bullets and the trouble were not mine this time, I leaned against a small pecan tree and counted the minutes to my next race, thrilled by how much better victory would taste if my daddy didn't arrive. Gnats circled my sweaty face and ice-cold orange juice dripped from my chin onto the shiny stainless-steel watch I'd received from Coach Mitchell as an early 11th birthday present. I wiped its face clean and confirmed that it was past eleven o'clock and that my daddy was late.

More than 350 students sat up in the bleachers and down on the grass in small clusters next to their respective teachers. In a large circle marked off by orange cones, the drum line from Durkeeville High School's marching band pounded out near-perfect covers of several popular songs. School administrators, dressed in matching embroidered polo shirts and khakis, gossiped behind cupped hands.

Some of the girls in my class executed a few of the latest dances while most of the boys poked fun at them. One silly Caucasian boy named Trip entertained another section of the coffee-colored crowd by jerking his body in a Harlem Shake.

"January."

I squinted to dilute the rare sunlight shining behind my friend Earl Brown. He stood biceps flexed and gap-toothed. "What's up?"

"Feel my muscle."

"Man, go 'head on."

Earl relaxed his pose and slapped my hand five. "Is your daddy coming?"

"I hope not."

"I'll bet you anything you want that I beat you today." Earl was a gambler by nature.

"Now and Laters and a bag of chips, 'cause I'm hungry."

Earl shook my hand to seal the deal and pulled me away from the tree. I stroked the waves in my hair with the small brush that lived in my pocket as we walked in the direction of my play-play sister Cindy Hightower and the other fine girls.

Butterflies fluttered inside my stomach, but I wasn't nervous about racing Earl or about talking to the girls. I doubled over and rubbed my midsection.

"What's wrong?"

"I've been meaning to ask you something," I said.

"What's wrong, man?" Earl looked ready to call an ambulance. "What is it?"

I rubbed my ribs and leaned backwards. "It ain't serious like that. I just get a li'l sick feeling when I think about it."

"Think about what?"

I grabbed Earl by both arms. "Does your daddy do drugs…or drink beer like there's no tomorrow?"

"Don't know."

"You don't know?"

Earl kicked the dirt at his feet. "I ain't ever met him."

Coach Swift trotted by and swatted each of us against the head. "No kissing in public, ladies," he said.

"Coach, you always trying to be funny," Earl said, and I laughed.

"Well then go take your mark for the fifty-yard dash," Coach said.

I jogged to the starting blocks; Earl, Trip and the rest of the competition followed. I tightened the laces on my all-white Nike cross-trainers and dug in. I was anxious to devour my winnings and jumped the gun twice before settling in.

Coach Swank, on the other end of the field, yelled, "On your mark, get set, *go*."

I exploded out of the starting block quicker than a hand moving away from a hot stove.

I heard screaming, cheering, and then, loudest of all, laughter. I remained calm, as I was taught to do in all endeavors, focusing on the end result—in this case, the finish line.

My ego told me that I was leading the pack, but what was funny about that? Curiosity spoiled my concentration, and I looked across my right shoulder.

There he was; two yards short of being parallel to me, in the dusty unpaved area about ten yards to the right of the grassy area that the coaches had converted into a track for the J. Russell Elementary School Annual Field Day.

Daddy C, my daddy, naked except for a pair of red nylon gym shorts emblazoned with the number 6 and hard-bottomed dress shoes, ran next to us coughing. His bare, hairy legs and face were covered in sweat. His head was thrown back, as if a parachute was slowing him. I pumped my arms harder and disappeared across the finish line. Daddy C and the rest of my fellow fifth graders were met at the line by a swirling tornado of cheers, dust, and humiliation.

To my surprise, I didn't stop running. I sprinted through the woods adjacent to the school, behind Happy Jacks Corner

Store–a place to purchase penny candy for a quarter and two-for-one malt liquor–and came upon Old Pappy Johnson's 1968 Chevrolet Impala. The semi-rusty classic sat bordered by tall sharp blades of green grass and red ants in Pappy's backyard, where the front yard used to be before the county changed the roads, and where Pappy had parked it before he lost his eyesight to glaucoma.

In the distance, teachers, coaches, and Daddy C called my name. The other children where still in an uproar. I understood why some of them hated on me–even to me it seemed that I won every contest or was the best in the school at this or that.

I was too embarrassed to face them and tugged on the passenger side door of the Chevy. I heard what sounded like a spring popping, and although the locking mechanism was in the down position, the door opened. I jumped in the back and lay on the floor, covering myself with a blanket smelling of kerosene, mildew, and old age.

Through small holes in the blanket, I saw pieces of some of the adults searching for me. Most walked right past the car, however, three of them leaned against the trunk and recounted how my father had once again managed to ruin an accomplishment of mine.

Daddy C's drug problem was much bigger than they'd calculated, they reasoned.

If they had asked, I would have confirmed.

Nevertheless, for all their intelligence and intuition, not a one of them ever looked through the window of the Chevy, where, I, January Calhoun III, hid for the rest of that day and the rest of my life.

CHAPTER ONE

Sam Jennings stepped towards me more irritated than concerned. "Mr. Calhoun, what are you talking about, now?"

"Where in the hell is my change? I need my change." I scratched the top of my head with all ten fingers. "The check was three ninety-four. I gave her a twenty-dollar bill."

Sam crossed his arms across his chest.

"I left my change sitting right here and that black ass waitress of yours done took my change 'cause I wouldn't give her a tip!"

"Come on Daddy C, are you sure about that? You were in the restroom the last ten minutes."

Seven Tennille rolled her eyes at Sam and moved towards me. "I didn't take your change, sir."

"Then where is it?"

I looked at Sam. "I been coming in here since my son was in the fifth grade." I swatted at the flies above my head and everyone looked at me as if I were hallucinating or something. "You don't value me as a customer?"

Seven threw her cleaning rag on the counter and untied her apron. "Man, you put the change in your back pocket."

"No, I didn't! I always put my paper dollars in my wallet and the change in my front left pocket." I patted my front left pocket and it didn't make a sound. I searched my wallet and it too was empty. "Now, what?"

"You didn't check your other back pocket!"

Frightened customers headed for the exits. Sam tried to run the register and temper the escalating argument. "Seven, darling, I won't fire you if you give the money back right now. We'll act like this never happened."

"It did 'never happen.' I can't believe you, Sam. I don't steal."

Sam saw it coming and didn't move fast enough.

Slap!

Seven threw her right hand across my face, and I didn't have time to blink. Sam grabbed her from behind.

I thought she was sobbing, but Seven scoured her mouth, gathering up phlegm, and spit it all into my face. The disgusting matter lay from my left eye across my nose.

With my limited set of conflict resolution skills, I was forced to beat the shit out of her.

I grabbed Seven by the arm, yanking her away from Sam. I punched her in the eye and mouth several times with my right fist. Blood slung from her face splashing onto everything in a three-foot radius.

When I let go of Seven's arm, she fell to the floor. I kicked her twice in the stomach. As I leaned over her body to strike her one last time, a police officer tackled me.

I scratched and clawed until I broke free from the officer's grasp. My lucky right hand hit the officer square on the jaw, giving me a chance to make a run for it. I burst through the front door and down the boulevard, leaving Seven lying on the floor with the sound of jingling bells ringing in her ears.

Bullets popped like firecrackers and ricocheted off the pavement. The cop screamed my name.

I kept running, digging a bigger hole for myself. Amazing grace moved my feet and body in the correct cadence to avoid the pursuit. Raindrops washed away my footprints. The more I ran, the louder my heart beat, until it was the loudest sound of all.

The last time I ran this fast, I almost beat my son, January, III, racing at his fifth grade Field Day. Every detail was clear and precise, like watching a digital videodisc frame by frame. I heard bloodhounds barking that were not there. I thought of Kunta Kente and Nat Turner. I thought of my son speaking to me through a telephone on the other side of plated glass. I thought of all the brothers before me who were shot and asked questions later.

Damn, I better stop running, flashed through my mind.

I rounded the back of the convenience store and found a ten-foot tall concrete wall. I thought about scaling it. Thank goodness my foolishness gave in to fatigue. I stopped, turned around, and threw up my hands to surrender.

That trick didn't work. The officer hit me in the ribs with his nightstick then across my shoulder. From the asphalt, I uncovered my eyes long enough to notice mean dark clouds as thick as mud pies outlining three or four angry officers. Shivering, they kicked and punched and hit on me until their nightsticks became waterlogged; while the bubblegum-chewing lieutenant stood there unfazed, reading me my Miranda rights.

"Sir, you are under arrest. You have the right to remain silent…"

Since I did have that right, and since I was tired, and since half of my face was swollen, the rest of the pompous cop's words fell upon deaf ears.

My khaki-colored Everett Hall suit now had crimson accents. My head began to sweat, and with the perspiration came an incredible itch that I was forced to suffer through because my hands were handcuffed behind my back.

Before they shoved me into the backseat of the patrol car, the lieutenant frisked me and emptied the contents of my pockets. In a tan envelope he placed a beaten-up wallet, a pair of fingernail clippers, a pocket size copy of the Old Testament, a Bic lighter, $16 dollars, a nickel, and a penny.

CHAPTER TWO

I stretched across three rows of bleachers and flipped through the stack of college recruitment letters Coach H. had given me earlier while I waited on this white boy.

Tripper D. Ought bobbed his blond head and danced his way up the gymnasium sideline drumming a beat on the tiered wooden planks in the process, like we had all the time in the world to do this.

"Hurry up and get this package, my nigga." I said, and then looked to see if anyone was watching.

"Everything's all right," Trip said. "Give me a second."

Four of my cuter female classmates walked by, startling us. "Hello, January. Good game the other night." I'm not sure which one gave me the compliment.

"Okay. Thanks... I'll see y'all a li'l later." I cleared my throat. "See, that's why I got to leave this mess alone quick. Half the time I'm paranoid as hell."

"What time is it? And you made like, six hundred dollars, already. We ain't been to calculus class yet. Why you complaining?"

"Whatever."

Trip fished around in his book bag. "If you quit, then you mess up my money, too."

"Is that supposed to mean something to me?"

"It better. Five pounds a week is a lot of work left undone," he mumbled.

"Who the hell you think you talking to?" I yanked him by his coat collar and pulled hard on a fistful of his long pretty hair. "You work these halls for me, not the other way around."

I pulled harder on his hair. "Stop, Boss. That shit hurts!" he said.

"I can have you expelled, arrested or placed in the lost and *unfound*," I reminded Trip. I relaxed the grip on his hair and let it slip through my fingers as he straightened himself.

I brushed off his shoulders and patted his head. "Now let's get on with it."

He handed me seven wrinkled $100 bills. "Here it is right here, B. My bad."

I removed the one-pound package from my book bag and shoved it inside the opening of his jacket, hard against his ribs, and hugged his back with my left arm.

"Let's get out of here," I said.

Trip entered the calculus class a few moments before I did and sat in the back. I walked through the door as the bell sounded beginning third period. I missed this class through the Christmas holidays, like Weight Watcher's miss cakes, cookies, and pies. In fact, I missed all my classes during our winter break. School is my vacation from life.

"This is it people, January seventh and the beginning of your last semester of your senior year. In a few more months it'll be you against the world," said Dr. H, our overqualified math teacher and boys' basketball coach. "Will you be ready?"

Man, please, I thought. Dr./Coach Leroy Herman Hawk is one of the smartest black people that I know exist, true enough. He'd once challenged that if anyone asked him a question–a math problem or any other question–to which he did not know the answer, the individual would receive an automatic A in his class without completing another assignment.

But he didn't know jack about my years at the school of hard knocks. I lived with my crack cocaine-addicted daddy in my grandmother's olive oil-anointed house, growing up alone in a metropolitan-sized city that was both urban and rural, somehow Ghetto and country, all at once. Like city folk the people in my neighborhood listen to hip-hop music and dream of Cadillac trucks, and like country folk we relish in our old ways. My first-grade teacher was my daddy's first-grade teacher.

With more blacks per capita than any other city in Florida, I often go weeks without seeing any white people, except for the insurance man and Trip, both of whom were grandfathered into our enclave.

The patch of land we call home is a polluted hope-deprived 20 blocks of cracked pavement and weed-infested lawns on the chocolate side of the interstate in the bowels of Jacksonville. Known by Rand McNally as Durkeeville, crates of returnable soda bottles and rusted metal washtubs sit in small backyards under fruit trees behind houses built 70 years ago. Overcast skies govern our community and our attitudes, unlike the bright sunshine that tourist brochures proclaim illuminates the rest of Florida.

Our neighborhood is surrounded by niggas and chaos, which might be redundant, but it's true. Every three or four nights, I toss and turn to the sound of knees and elbows wrestling for space against pecan shells and autumn dried leaves while cheap prostitutes put in work behind the house.

Inside the house, Daddy C taught me to only trust him and God, and that's what I did. Daddy C is not my biological father, as dysfunctional families are not exclusive to black people; but they both are all that I know. Some cat that I do not know helped my mother conceive me. Daddy C was my mother's husband at the time she became pregnant and was not told the truth about me until I was four years old. Thank God he never unleashed his anger on me. Underneath it all he is my best friend. Not in the sense that we hang out together or take long walks and talk, but he's the friend who most wants the best for me. To him, and to me, I am his son.

I suppose, my mother was a little "out there," but she's still my mama. This, as time goes on, is more and more unfortunate because I haven't seen her since I was nine years old. On the two occasions that I asked Daddy C of her whereabouts, I was spanked and told that she moved. That was it–"she moved."

Grandma–Sister Betty to you–is my maternal grandmother, Daddy C's mother-in-law. All three of us live in a big two-story house on Columbine Drive off Myrtle Avenue.

We have small hairy four-legged roommates during the winter and bold nocturnal cockroaches hosting sleepovers during the summer. One of the prayers that I pray every night is that I don't step on or get stepped on by one of our uninvited houseguests.

Cindy Hightower is the one guest who I was allowed to have visit our house. She and her parents lived across the street from us. At first we argued over who could run faster, then beat up people for each other, and finally graduated to giving the other their first kiss.

But, it takes a lot of wood to keep a love affair that started at nine years old kindling. Cindy and I agreed that the long-term effects of our friendship should outweigh our elementary love affair. We decided to be friends, or more exactly, I claimed her as my little sister and she crowned me her big brother.

Besides playing sports and reading books, my childhood was spent wishing I were grown up. After enduring 50 years of life during my first 17 years here on Earth–"grown up" is what I now consider myself to be.

"Dr. H., why you talk like that?" Trip asked.

"How do you prefer that I speak?" Most of the class laughed.

"I'm just saying, you always trying to talk proper. Why you can't just talk black?"

Dr. H. rubbed his hands together and tugged on the bottom of his orange Leroy Selmon Tampa Bay Bucs throwback jersey, but I was confident he would have an answer.

"And you, the lone European male in this school, are an authority on that topic?"

My li'l sister Cindy rolled her eyes at me, in part because Dr. H. had a legitimate question and two, because she didn't like me fooling with Trip. She didn't trust him.

"Sir, you're avoiding the question. Do I smell an A in your class?" Trip asked.

"Ain't no gas in it!" The class cracked up again. "Okay. You say that I 'talk proper.' What is proper?"

"I don't know. I'm just saying–"

Dr H. slapped his hand on Trip's desk. "No. When you asked me, what did you mean?"

"It's kinda like always trying to correct somebody."

Dr. H. walked to the front of the room and spun to face us, using some type of heel-toe maneuver.

"Well, let's say that your definition is right. In order to correct something, it has to first be what?"

"Wrong," the class said in unison.

Dr. H. pointed at Trip. "And if you change something from being wrong it is now what?"

"Right," Trip answered.

"So your question was 'why do I talk proper, why can't I just talk black.' Basically you said to me 'why you always trying to be right, why can't you just be wrong?' "

Trip offered the same lame response he always did when he realized that he better give up the fight. "I hear what're you saying, but…"

The class hollered, and some of us slapped high fives as controlled disorder covered the room.

"Damn, Dr. H.!" Cindy said.

"Bet that. And watch your mouth, li'l mama." Everybody laughed at his obvious attempt to sound hip.

"I apologize, Dr. H.," Trip said.

"I feel you. I've often been tried, never denied, and willing to be tried, again."

Thinking about Trip's audacity to challenge Dr. H. further solidified my desire to end our business relationship. He's book smart, but lacks the thought process to survive. You have to pick your battles. He should have known that this was one he couldn't win.

Dr. H. smiled and got back to business.

"Now, has anyone received his SAT scores?"

A few people raised their hands, but I didn't want to talk about it.

"I did, Dr. H. I made a thousand," Earl Brown blurted out.

"That's respectable."

"I got twelve sixty," Trip bragged, causing Cindy to break her promise to keep my business private.

"Dr. H., January scored a perfect 1600!"

Everyone in the class looked at me with their mouths open not making a sound. God, I was embarrassed. I hoped my niggas on the street wouldn't find out.

CHAPTER THREE

As I approached my last class for the day, Spanish IV, our teacher, Ms. Martinez, stood at the door with her arms crossed looking sexy as ever. I patted my hair and looked down to make sure my gear was in check. I wear my clothes like the majority of kids my age: shirts coordinated, layered and too big; sneakers or boots clean; pants ironed and sagging with me pulling them back up on my waist every fifth step I take.

"Pull your pants up, boy," she said.

"What's up, Ms. Martinez. Can I call you tonight?"

"You know you don't have my phone number."

"Oh, I have it. The Internet is the information superhighway. I'm just afraid to use the number."

"Your hair is always nice." Ms. Martinez searched my head for an out-of-place hair. She didn't find one. "Who is your barber? He must be a perfectionist."

"Mike O at GQ2," I moved closer towards her. "You can play in it any time you get ready."

"Back up Chico," Ms. Martinez unfolded her arms. "I don't want to lose my job and you don't want a sexual harassment charge."

"Ay, m*ami.*"

"*Vamanos.*" Ms. Martinez entered the classroom. "The bell is about to ring."

I took my usual spot in the back.

"Okay listen up, today we–" Ms. Martinez started.

"Ms. Martinez? Ms. Martinez, can you send January Calhoun to the office?" the school principal, Dr. Mitchell, said through the intercom system. I grabbed my book bag and headed to the office.

Cindy passed me in the hallway and apologized for revealing our secret. "I'm sorry about this morning."

"No pressure. They were going to find out sooner or later, I guess." I readjusted my book bag on my shoulder.

"Boss, I need to get a package from you."

"If I was going to let you do that, I'd tell you to go see Trip. But since I'm not, leave me alone about that li'l sis."

Cindy frowned. "You think you're my big brother for real. You're the 'Boss' of Durkeeville, but you're not the boss of me."

I waved her off. "Whatever. Right now I'm on the way to see Dr. Mitchell."

"Yeah? Must be serious. What's up?"

"Don't know yet," I said, "but don't run your mouth."

After surveying the area for police–I didn't see any–I entered the door of the front office. Dr. Mitchell met me at the front counter.

"Pull your pants up, boy," he said. I tugged on my Dickie work pants and smiled.

"What's up, Dr. Mitchell."

"Follow me to my office."

I sat in one of the three big comfortable leather chairs as Dr. Mitchell closed the door behind me.

"January, I'm concerned about your father. On the outside, dressed up in his suits… Did you know that he used to come to the games dressed like that the year we won the state championship?"

"Yes, he told me."

"I used him as an example for the other boys…valedictorian and everything, and now look at him."

"Good looking. He's a captivating person up until his fifth beer or third blunt, at which time you can expect to find him asleep or in trouble."

"January, stop it."

"No. I mean no, sir." I shook my head. "He runs the streets all day, and if he makes it home, he abuses his drug of choice for the day until he passes out."

"January, it'll get better."

"Some people are weaker on the inside than they look on the outside, Dr. Mitchell."

"I'm well aware of this; that's why I'm also concerned about you."

"Sir, you might see me get shaken up a li'l bit. You might see me lose," I leaned forward in my seat. "but you'll never see me give up."

Dr. Mitchell looked out of his office window and took a deep breath.

"You've seen too much, too much too soon. That's why I give you a pass for the mess you pull." Dr. Mitchell took a seat behind his desk. "You know you would've been expelled by now if you were anywhere else."

"Is that the only reason I get a pass?"

"Well, I guess your donations to the Gentlemen's Fund do serve to further your cause."

"Is *that* the only reason?" I asked.

"Son, you run this neighborhood. I run this school!"

"There's no need to get upset. We're both smart enough to realize that this school is within this neighborhood."

"Look, I didn't call you in here for this. I have some news for you."

Dr. Mitchell rose from his chair then sat on the edge of his desk, next to his orange Florida A&M University baseball cap, and placed his hand on my shoulder. "I have another test of your resolve, son."

What is it this time, I thought.

"It seems that Daddy C walked into Sam's Diner this morning, high as a kite, and nearly beat that cute little waitress, Seven to death. The police have him at the station right now. Sister Betty called and told me."

This wasn't major news to me. It was singular only because Daddy C had been *caught* doing something while he was high on some type of drug. I remained quiet.

"If Daddy C doesn't chill, people are going to think he's that serial killer around town." Dr. Mitchell peered through the horizontal blinds. "Your father certainly isn't your average crack head…"

"And I'm not your average crack head's son. To whom much is given, much is expected, Dr. Mitchell. I don't like it, either, but I can handle it."

I grabbed my bag and headed for the door. I sensed that Dr. Mitchell wouldn't try to stop me. He didn't know if he had said too much or not enough.

I didn't go downtown to the station or go by to see my grandmother. I forgot all about basketball practice. Cindy's cousin is on the team, and I was sure she'd tell him about my meeting with the principal.

If I were a cartoon character, I would crawl into the ground. Instead, I went to the one place no one had ever been able to find me–my '68 Chevy I kept parked in front of Pappy Johnson's house–and closed my eyes in the backseat.

CHAPTER FOUR   *January 7ᵗʰ*

Dear Chevy,

It's me January. You wouldn't believe how many journals are tucked under your front seat. It's a good thing I always keep the current one under the driver-side floor mat.

This year has started like the last one left off. We won another basketball game, I scored a bunch of points, and Daddy C embarrassed me again. We beat Robert Jerome High by thirty-two points. The paper said I scored 40. I shoot the ball a lot; I can't keep up with the points.

Daddy C beat the mess out of the waitress at the diner. I'm sure he had no idea Seven was my girlfriend. She's a college student, twenty-one years old, a country girl with a big heart. We met a year and a half ago and I've loved her since the first day I saw her. She's working at the diner to make the money I give her look legit. Daddy C doesn't know any of that because he doesn't know me.

Come to think of it, Seven doesn't know that he's my daddy. At least, <u>I didn't tell her</u>. I haven't decided if I'm visiting him or not. He knows more people in town than the mayor. There's a good chance that he'll be out of jail before I get there.

Why thousands of people stand behind an unabashed drug abuser is beyond me. In the Bible, there came a time where Peter asked the Lord, "How often shall my brother sin against me, and I forgive him?" Peter thought that seven times would be sufficient. But Jesus said unto him, "Not seven times, but seventy times seven."

I'm telling you; Daddy C has used up about 481 of his chances.

Don't know what I'd do without you

Love,
January III

CHAPTER FIVE   *January 30th*

Dear Chevy,

It's your boy. It's been a few weeks since we've talked. I noticed some icicles hanging from your side view mirrors. It's always harder to open your door this time of year. I'm a little under the weather today, too.

Why do otherwise rational people, continue to participate in activities that don't make sense? I know that I'm a strong person, because at the end of the day I'm still standing, but I'm starting to hate myself for my weaknesses.

I'm involved in things I don't want to do anymore, with people I'm not certain I ever liked. My day job pays, but I know it's not an honorable profession. I put $100,000 in to investments that don't hold water, morally. I've stacked $437,000 in two years that I'm sitting on, literally. I started hustlin' because I wanted crisp jeans and diamond jewelry like the people I saw on MTV. Grandma's fixed income was broken down and accounted for to the penny; none of which was allocated to me. Daddy C couldn't exactly afford to purchase that stuff for me on his drug addict's salary. Now I have all that, and plenty of cash, but no peace of mind. Why can't I stop?

At least college is covered. I can't depend on them white people to give me a scholarship. I might have grades and play ball and all that, but they be acting funny sometime.

Daddy C didn't get out of jail for twenty-one days! Can you believe it? It looked as if he might get punished for <u>this</u> crime, then out of nowhere Seven dropped the charges. She's all better now, healed up and everything, as beautiful as ever. She's also driving a new Honda Accord that neither of us paid for.

Do you think Daddy C dried himself or sobered up while he was in jail? Do you think Pappy Johnson ever sees me get into this car?

Glad we could spend this time together

Love,

January III

CHAPTER SIX

"Hello. Hello. This is your daddy," I said into January's cellular voice mail during a five-minute break. "Pick up the...call me back at this number."

I've been out of jail for three weeks. The officer I struck was an old friend from elementary school who said that my bruised ribs made us even. I had no business putting my hands on that pretty little girl, and I regret it. My good friend and former mentor Coach Mitchell put in a word on my behalf, and the young lady found the goodness in her heart to forgive me for my trespasses.

"January, it's me again. Wanted to let you know that I signed up for a drug treatment program at Noah's House. Ah...call me back."

We meet at Noah's House every Monday evening. Once inside, we're shepherded into certain seats to subtlety encourage group participation. I can't get into it, yet. My usual practice is to sit; act annoyed, and watch, through the shattered window glass, the last of rush-hour traffic weave its way home.

Water drips from the window unit a/c onto the concrete floor and runs down the length of the baseboards in a pale blue haze. It reminds me of the ice-cold air blowing inside the last automobile that I owned, a '94 Nissan Maxima.

Everyone else in this drab converted pool hall was either ordered by the courts or coerced by a family member into coming here. There are eight of them in all, not counting myself, and including the facilitator of the meeting–nine people trying to take 12 steps.

One of them motioned to another in my direction. They both nodded.

"What's up?" the taller one wearing the nice pair of Johnston & Murphy's said. "You're Daddy C, aren't you?"

I didn't answer.

I thought it over and realized that the first step might be the hardest for me to take. To admit that I was powerless over *anything* and that my life had become unmanageable was too much for me to agree to.

I always envisioned a group like this to sit in circles holding hands under bright lights. I figured everyone who left here was the better for having come. This place was nothing like I thought it would be, and I wasn't putting in enough effort for it to be beneficial.

Every meeting started the same. The leader of the group would welcome everyone then inform us of a statistic that was intended to comfort us in our struggles with our addictions.

"Approximately six point two million Americans age twelve or older have tried crack cocaine at least once in their lifetime," he'd say.

Yes, it did help to know that I was not alone, but I couldn't adjust to the therapy. By the time the symbolic microphone had been passed around this jagged edged circle and the group assumed it was my turn to speak, for the third week in a row, I wasn't feeling it. My right leg bounced to its own drum, as usual. I closed my eyes and rubbed my mouth with my hand and shook my uninterested head. I looked out of the window, into the darkness, and mumbled to my pitiful self.

When I decided to open my mouth, I interrupted the group laughing at a joke that I didn't understand.

"Excuse me. Excuse me, everyone," I said.

"He speaks," the facilitator of the meeting cracked.

The group laughed at that remark as if they wanted to laugh at me about *something* for weeks.

"Whatever. I wanted to let y'all know that I'm leaving."

To my surprise, and a little to my disappointment, no one tried to stop me.

I walked halfway up the block and called my old friend State Representative Rodney James. Congressman James was in town on business until Wednesday.

"May I speak to Ra-Ra," I said.

"Who is this? This must be somebody from the old neighborhood."

"What's up, Congressman? It's January Calhoun."

"Daddy C? Man, how you doing?" he asked. "I've heard some things about you, you know, and they ain't all been good. How did you get my cell phone number?"

"You know if tell one nigga something, it's like you told them all."

"How did you know I was in town?"

"Man, I'm having a few problems these days, but I'm still the mayor of these here streets." I inched closer to the pay phone, trying to suppress the road noise to make Rodney think I owned a cell phone.

"Are you busy right now, Rodney?"

"Not exactly. Why?"

"Come pick me up, man. I'm on Main Street. You'll recognize me; I'm the only nigga down here wearing an Armani suit."

"Some things never change, huh?" he asked. "I've got my little lady, LeAndra, with me. We'll have to make a stop before we can do anything."

"That's fine."

"I'm not too far from you; be there in a minute."

Around 7:45 P.M., Rodney and LeAndra picked me up on the corner of Eighth and Main, a few blocks away from The Sheik restaurant which specialized in steak and pita bread "Camel Rider" sandwiches and one block from the old converted pool hall. Rodney, his lady, and the rented silver Jaguar all contradicted the immediate environment like good news in this area of drugs, prostitution, and lost hope. I slid in the backseat cooler than a fan.

"Hello, beautiful, my name is January." I extended my hand over the back of the seat. The warmth and softness of LeAndra's reminded me of one of my women.

"What's up, Daddy C," Rodney said, interrupting my instant fascination with LeAndra.

Rodney headed on up Main St. and jumped on the Twentieth Street Expressway traveling west. In another minute, we were on I-95 North headed to the Northside.

That area of town reminds me of Atlanta: dark brown, progressive, and prosperous. There is plenty of good food to eat, although every spot seems to be take-out, complete with bulletproof windows, burglar bars on all of the deadbolt locked doors, and rude unapologetic order takers who act as if they have somewhere better to be.

I wasn't sure where we were going. LeAndra and Rodney took turns staring at each other while Rodney drove up the road. Each time, one would say to the other, "what is it?" then they laughed or shared a quick kiss, like only people who are in love can get away with. I closed my eyes to take a nap.

When I awoke, LeAndra was long gone, having already boarded her flight to Tampa. Rodney and I were in front of the Platinum Kitty Kat.

The Kat is an unadulterated, anything-goes strip club. Certified by the State of Florida and AAA, the Platinum Kitty Kat is a Jacksonville landmark. It's fun and exciting and yet, common and regular. The place is bright and inviting on the outside, cold and dim on the inside, and for an institution of its kind, it's safer than most.

"Oh, you came to the right place," I said, "but take me back up the road to get a quart of beer. I can't go up in there sober."

Rodney shifted the car into reverse, and we headed to the Li'l Champ convenience store at the next light.

I went inside and bought 64 ounces of Schlitz malt liquor for $2.00; about a dollar cheaper than the same amount of vitamin D enriched whole milk.

This time I slid into the front seat, still cooler than a fan. I gave half of the beer to Rodney, and I didn't even blink to give him a head start. We both took it straight to the head, rekindling an old game we used to play to see who finished the quart of beer first.

I won, of course. Congressman Rodney James is dignified and a casual drinker. I, on the other hand, am serious about my hobbies and refuse to be outdone by anyone.

We drove back to the club. I killed the miniature bottle of Courvoisier I had in my coat pocket, and we went inside. At the door, an attractive Caucasian girl with a tongue ring and two tattoos recognized me right away and gave me a big hug.

The big fat guy with SECURITY splashed across his chest checked our pockets and scanned us for weapons.

"We don't want any mess out of you, Daddy C," he said.

"Hold that down, my nigga. I'm in good company tonight. Everything will be fine."

I gave him the twenty-dollar cover charge. He said for me to keep it, that it might be my last bit of money or some shit. I let him think whatever he wanted. I hit the number today for a $1,000, but there was no need to mention all that.

We proceeded past fifteen of the finest women in Florida, all either sitting on stools or standing by the bar preying on unsuspecting customers.

Once inside the stage area of the club, my heart began to race. The music grabbed me by the foot and did not let go. The Florida-style hip-hop, consisting of catchy sing-along type of rhymes coupled with loud trunk-rattling bass programmed at ninety-eight beats per minute, was always more about the party than the battle, more about the fun than the struggle. Real rapping was what the ladies' men did, not over-thugged-out teenagers narrating dreams.

The music boomed from the multitude of speakers placed in the corners or hanging from overhead. Two light-skinned women were on stage gyrating, shaking what their mamas gave them. Three others worked the crowd for lap dances or private shows or both. If you enjoyed liquor or wine, it flowed from the bar like water. If you preferred your cocaine soft, no problem, it rose out of tables like large anthills.

"So what's going on with you, these days?" Rodney asked.

"Man, let me tell you…" I stirred my drink with a straw. "Shit, I really don't know, I can't tell you."

Rodney shook the ice in his glass and rubbed the sides of his mouth and then his chin. "Well, what about your son?"

"He's the best child a parent could ask for—straight A's, athlete, and everything… I don't even know him anymore."

"You two don't live together?"

"That's why it don't make no sense. We live with Sister Betty over on Columbine Drive."

"How is Sister Betty?"

"She's fine. She does a lot of volunteering at Head Start."

"That's good, glad to hear that," he said. "What happened to your wife, Dru?"

"Put it like this: good looks are an asset, but in a long-term relationship what a brother *needs* is someone he can talk to." I was upset that he even mentioned her name. "And by that I mean that she would be an accomplished *listener!*"

Rodney took a sip of his Crown Royal and Coke. "Amen."

"I needed a woman who was secure enough to let my wants and needs supercede her own, because then it would have been hard for me not to reciprocate that kind of dedication."

"I feel you," Rodney said.

I felt liberated talking about my pathetic life. I needed this, somebody to listen to me who knew the old me, with all my promise and potential.

Rodney nodded.

"I wasn't proud of her parenting skills, either."

"What do you mean?"

"I don't know if I should tell you this…one time…I don't even want to get into it."

"It's that bad?" Rodney said.

"It's a shame, is what it is."

"I wanted her to be like my grandmother." I took a long sip of my Courvoisier. "I would have settled for her being like my mama, but she wanted to grab the rebound, pass the ball to herself, and take all the shots."

"Speaking of basketball, do you still shoot it a li'l bit?"

"I can spin the ball on my index finger for a long time, but..." I shrugged.

"I read that your son broke your state scoring record. Is he going to join you in the Florida Hall of Fame or does he just shoot the ball a lot?"

I perked up a little. "When January was ten years old at Punt, Pass, and Kick, right? He goes first and throws a perfect spiral fifty-one yards down the field."

"No he didn't."

"Yes, he did. I'm trying to tell you."

Rodney raised his eyebrows. "Nobody else even wanted to try after that."

"I wouldn't either," he said.

I finished my Courvoisier and motioned for the waitress to bring me another. "January's damn good, on a very good team, but the boy shoots the ball so much, the rest of the guys are as anonymous as Motown's Funk Brothers–"

"Excuse me, gentlemen, can me and my girl do a table dance for you? It's only five dollars apiece," this tall curvaceous beauty with long flowing hair cascading against mocha-colored skin, flashing her perfect teeth, said.

Rodney grinned from ear to ear. "You sure can."

The girls made me forget all about my recent troubles. They moved to the beat in synchronized perfection. I liked when they made their butt cheeks clap.

Those fine bodies and loud music distracted Rodney and me. It was a pleasant distraction, but disastrous, nonetheless.

The security guard asked the guy next to us to take his drink off the pool table. He seemed to have asked nice enough, I thought.

Again he said, "Please, for the last time, take your drink off the table, sir."

"Man, get out of my face." The guy stabbed the end of the pool stick into the floor. "If you ask me that one more time, it's on."

"Can you read the letters on my shirt?" the security guard asked. "They're there for a reason."

My man decided to take the drink off the pool table, but threw it in the guard's face.

The security guard wiped his face once to clear his field of vision then chased the youngster halfway around the table. The guard had quick feet for a man his size. When people started laughing, the young boy stopped running and put his hands up to fight.

The guard grabbed the youngster by his oversized NBA jacket, and threw him on the ground. He punched the young fella four times in the face, kicked him twice in the stomach then hit him across the back with a pool stick.

The music stopped.

The security guard yelled, "I tried to tell you."

The dancers cleared the area, racing for the dressing rooms. Most of the patrons headed for the front door. Rodney grabbed my arm and motioned for us to dip out of the rear emergency exit. It was a good idea, but very poor timing. We opened the door to the exit, and the alarm sounded, adding Tabasco sauce to an already heated situation.

Two masked gunmen rushed in through the same door we'd opened. They started firing bullets in every direction. One of them grabbed the security guard and hit him across the temple with his gun.

Another one hollered, "Nobody move."

They shot up the mirrors and the lights. I couldn't figure out if the gun play was retaliation for the young boy getting beat up or if it was a planned robbery and their timing was as bad as Rodney's.

The congressman turned around to run, and one of the gunmen shot him in the leg.

I was high on cocaine and full of liquid courage. I'll use temporary insanity as my excuse for lunging at the shooter and screaming, "Have you lost your damn mind?"

That boy had a scar in the shape of a lightning bolt on his neck that stretched within an inch of his right collarbone. He shot me six times and each time I saw flashes of light. He hit me once in the chest, three times in the stomach, and when I fell to the floor, he shot twice in the leg. I landed perpendicular, across Rodney's body. People started running again and somebody stepped on my injured leg.

"Are you alright?" Rodney asked.

"I didn't feel the bullets, but I saw my body jerking," I said. "Are you okay?"

"He got me in my right thigh, but I'll be all right. Be quiet and lay there. It'll all be over in a minute."

Blood spilled out of me like water out of a ruptured hose. "I'm a beat that boy's ass when I learn who he is. You'll see."

CHAPTER SEVEN

According to the round clock on the pale concrete wall, we arrived at the emergency room at 4:00 A.M. I prepared myself for the torture. To pass the time, I drafted two lists. The first one consisted of possible ailments or injuries that constituted an "emergency." Judging from our three-hour wait, my grandmother's swelling in her right knee, shortness of breath, and severe headache did not qualify.

Paramedics brought in patients with varying medical needs and proceeded past us in the waiting game. We didn't arrive by ambulance; I carried Grandma into the triage area. We were told to sign in, have a seat, and that someone would be with us soon.

My second list recorded all the possible time frames and definitions of "soon."

This exercise in time mismanagement should have been avoided. I knew what was wrong with her; however, she needed to hear it from someone older than myself, someone white, or someone wearing a white doctor's jacket.

Grandma suffers from diabetes and high blood pressure, like most black people who grew up eating cereal, syrup sandwiches, and fried pork chops.

She has medicine and a diet plan to help control both of her problems. She won't follow her regimen, though, unless somebody is home to make her do it. She can't count on me because I'm not trying to be around Columbine Drive. I spend the least amount of time there as possible. I put in a little work in the neighborhood, eat a few meals there, sleep there, and that's about it.

When the nurse called for Grandma, we both were asleep. I jumped up; Grandma was slow to wake. I moved her ever-present Bible from her lap and helped her up.

The nurse looked to be about my age. She was small with a cute shape and green eyes.

"Hello, Mrs. Knight. Have a seat here, and I'll wheel you in to see the doctor."

"Hi," I said.

"Hi. Don't I know you?"

"I'm not sure, sweetheart. I apologize. I don't remember you."

The three of us entered an even colder room that reeked of rubbing alcohol. Again, we were told to wait.

"Hold on, now. We've been here for hours, already. I have school in a few minutes…we've got the state championship game tonight…"

"That's it. You're that basketball player who's made straight A's and never missed a day of school," the nurse said. "I read about you in the paper. Nice photo, too."

"That's me, but I'm tired. We're tired. Can you have the doctor hurry it up, please? Thank you. I'm sorry if I sound rude."

Grandma squeezed my hand and smiled.

"January," she said. "What does it say in Genesis thirty-seven, verse five?"

"Grandma, I'm too tired to play Scriptures. Plus, I might be a li'l rusty."

"Once the Word is in your heart, it's always in your heart," she said.

"Grandma–"

"You have ten seconds," she said.

I sighed and scratched under my chin then answered. "And Joseph dreamed a dream and he told it his brethren: and they hated him yet more."

"Ah yes," Grandma said. She loved playing this game with me. "The dreamless always despise the dreamer."

She patted my hand. "What about Romans one seventeen?"

"Um, let me see," I said. "For therein is the righteousness of God revealed from faith to faith: as it is written, THE JUST SHALL LIVE BY FAITH."

"That's right. What one believes *does* make a difference."

At that moment the doctor walked in. "Mrs. Knight?" he said.

"Hello doctor. Give me one minute, please." Grandma looked at me. "This one is worth fifty points. What are Philippians three, twelve and thirteen?"

"Fifty points? You know that means if I get it right you owe me a sweet potato pie."

"Fifty points," she said.

I cleared my throat. "Not as though I had already attained, either were already perfect: but I follow after, if that I may apprehend that for which also I am apprehended of Christ Jesus." I paused before finishing my answer.

The doctor winked at me and when I began the second verse he joined in with me. "Brethren, I count not myself to have apprehended: but *this* one thing I do, forgetting those things which are behind, and reaching forth unto those things which are before," we said in unison.

Grandma was clearly impressed with us both and listened intently as the doctor told her what she refused to hear me say. He admonished her to "eat right or die fast," and we were on our way.

The same nurse discharged us.

"Your name's January, right?"

"Yes, that's right."

"I get off soon–at eight thirty. If you don't make it to class, call me at this number." She slid me her name and telephone number.

I read her name from the business card and looked up. "Well, Jasmine, I will be making it to class. Like you said, I never miss school. Is it okay if I use this number some other time?"

"This afternoon before the game, next week, two months from now. . . I don't care when. Yes." She giggled. "And Mrs. Knight, please take care of yourself, girl. We want to talk with you, not about you."

"My God shall supply all my needs," Grandma replied.

Calvin the Cabbie, our personal taxi driver, took us back to the house. I made sure that Grandma had everything she needed and had Calvin rush me to school.

Trip and three of his friends met me at the front entrance of the school.

"Slow down, B, you've got six minutes before the first bell rings," Trip said. "We need six of those packages, Boss."

"Who are these people?" I asked.

"They go to All Saints private school on the Westside."

I looked at the three fellas and figured they must be ball players because not that many black six-four niggas went to private school.

"So what do they want from me?"

"They want to move a few packages."

"Do I look like UPS or FEDEX or something?"

"Very funny, Boss. Why you trippin'?" Trip said.

"What is your name again, white boy?" I said.

"Oh, so now you don't know me?"

"I don't know what you're talking about, white boy, but if you say another word I'm a have to embarrass you in front of your friends." I shook Trip's hand then looked at the three fellas. "You shouldn't believe everything you hear."

I entered the school and never looked back.

Dennis Ryan, the senior class clown, read the morning announcements across the school closed circuit television outlet as I walked into first period sociology class.

"What's up, Mr. Richards. Am I on time?"

"Yes. Have a seat."

I made my way to the back of the class, center aisle, last seat; the same seat I occupied in all my classes.

"What's up," my classmates said.

"What's up," I responded to everybody in my row.

"...And don't forget that tonight the boys' basketball team returns to the Lakeland Civic Center for the state championship. We need everybody there to support the team. We have seven charter buses reserved; you can purchase your tickets from yours truly or from any of the other Sixth Man Club members," Dennis said. "But don't give your money to Trip; he might smoke it up–I mean, he might misplace it."

"Jessica, turn that TV off. Dennis Ryan is liable to say anything when he gets on the air," Mr. Richards directed. He laughed a little then turned his mouth up and looked me in the eye.

"Mr. Calhoun, congratulations on your success, and I hope you all win tonight, but Mr. Ryan reminded me of something...how do you feel about teenagers and drug use?"

The entire class turned around to hear my response. I volleyed with a Serena Williams return.

"My personal experience has been with adult drug abuse, and if adulthood is the elevation of adolescence in most occurrences of life, then I would say that it is best that a teenager not be associated with drugs."

The class refocused their attention on the teacher, being sure not to look him in the eye because they didn't want to have to contribute to the discussion. At one time or another, some more than others, most of them were customers of mine, even if I had only sold them a few of Daddy C's beers.

Mr. Richards unfolded his arms and prepared to speak, but I interrupted.

"Especially not if you look like me," I said. "We all know that drug activity is color blind, but drug law enforcement is not. These drug enforcement agents prey on areas like this."

I stood and pointed at the window. "They're probably out there by the park right now, dressed up as prostitutes or transients, watching every move our black behinds make."

"Would you say that you have always felt that way, or is this a new opinion of yours?" Mr. Richards asked.

"Sir, I'm speaking facts. Five times as many black men will go to prison in their lifetime as white men. These other kids in this classroom can tell you that I've been catching hell behind someone's drug usage since I was in the third grade. Why would you...no, this is not a new opinion."

This was one of my favorite classes because Mr. Richards didn't follow a curriculum and anything could be discussed and fit under the realm of "the study of society, social institutions, or social relationships."

"I know a little about your troubles with your father. I hate to say it, but who doesn't? Without getting personal, does anyone want to offer a suggestion as to how a person can hurt someone they care for or is it that men in the American society are unable to show affection?" Mr. Richards said to the class.

I sat down in my chair then took my headphones off and placed my portable CD player in my book bag.

"Mr. Richards, they don't have to talk for me," I said.

"Then go ahead, Mr. Calhoun."

"Men are capable of love. Look at these guys in fraternities or male best friends. They will lie, fight, or cheat for each other. They keep secrets and bail each other out of jams." I grabbed an orange from my bag and began to peel it. "A dude can be pissed off at his best friend, but will fight for him at the drop of a hat if necessary."

"Okay, I'll give you those points, but why can't y'all seem to do the same with females?" Tara Jackson interjected.

"That's because guys know a little secret about girls."

"Tell 'em about it, January," Dennis Ryan tossed in, having finally made it back to class.

"The secret is that girls love guys conditionally," I said.

"Now wait a minute, January. You might get something started in here," Mr. Richards said, in his usual instigative way.

I put two orange slices in my mouth. "Hear me out, Mr. Richards."

"Yeah, Mr. Richards, I need to hear *this*," Tara said.

Mr. Richards went to his desk and snickered, his job done for the hour.

"I'll let Earl Brown borrow a hundred dollars for something real important, even though he already owes me fifty from last month. But women aren't like that. I don't know."

"I'm not feeling you. Make me understand," Cindy, my ubiquitous, unsolicited mouthpiece, said.

"What I'm saying is…in my experience, girls are reactionary. If you don't have an attitude, she won't either. If you keep her hair and nails done, she will allow you to take her on a date to spend more money on her. If not–" I balled up the orange peel in a piece of paper and shot it into the wastebasket. "If you act right, according to her standards, then she'll give you a little, a little…you know what I'm saying."

"No one in here is having sex, right?" Mr. Richards asked. The entire class laughed, even the virgins.

"Those are examples, but if any of those 'conditions' are not satisfied, she'll show you her true colors." I stood to take off my jacket. "Your boys and your parents love you unconditionally, that's it. You go to jail for manslaughter and your mama will say it was self-defense; your boys will say you were framed. Your girl will say that you should've kept your butt home that day."

"They won't say *butt*, they'll say *your dumb ass*," that fool Dennis Ryan said.

"Some of that makes sense, but are you insinuating that black females treat their men this way and white girls make better wives?" Tara asked.

"What are you talking about? My grandma is black; I live in an all-black neighborhood and go to an all-black high school. Every female in this room right now is black." I shrugged and turned my palms up. "I don't know much about them crackers–"

"January…"

"My bad, Mr. Richards. I'm sorry, but what is this broad talking about?" The brothers in the class laughed.

"Am I talking about black women? Of course, I am. Am I talking about *all* black women? Hell, naw."

"January, calm down," Mr. Richards said.

"Let me just say this and I'll be quiet."

"Go ahead."

"I'll put it like this…y'all know my story." I looked to the left and then to the right. "Where in the hell is my mama? Why she ain't with my daddy? He wasn't good enough? What conditions didn't he meet?"

When no one answered, Mr. Richards rose from his chair and began to hand out our written assignment for the day. "I don't know why y'all wanted to get January Calhoun, III started today," he said.

"Actually, you started it Mr. Richards," Cindy said.

"Indeed, I did. My bad."

"Y'all act like y'all scared of January or something," Tara said.

"You watch your mouth, hear me?" Cindy jumped out of her chair and pointed at Tara. "That's my dog, can't nobody kick my dog, but me."

Tara rolled her eyes, but remained quiet.

For the remainder of the period everyone worked on his/her respective assignment until the bell sounded, cutting like a knife through the tension in the air. I sensed everyone felt that they were saved by it. The noise of the student body changing classes drowned Mr. Richards's homework instructions. Cindy met me outside in the hall.

"I had to take Grandma to the hospital early this morning," I said.

"Is she all right?"

"Yes, but hardheaded. Listen, I only came to school to play in the game tonight, to be on the roll." I flipped through my sociology book and then looked Cindy in the eye. "I got to stop moving these packages, you feel me."

"Yeah, that's cool. Let me have your last one whenever you retire." I could tell she didn't believe me.

I hugged her, then snuck into the staff lounge and out of their private back door and dialed seven numbers into my cell phone.

CHAPTER EIGHT

"Hello, may I speak to Jasmine?"

When she answered, "This is Jasmine," imagination brought a whiff of the sweet fragrances of her namesake to my nose.

"This is January Calhoun. You said that I could call you anytime."

"I did. What's going on?"

"I need you to pick me up and let me chill at your place for a few hours."

"Are you all right?"

"Fine. Pick me up, sweetheart. I'll be inside the Laundromat on the corner of Eighth Street and Myrtle Avenue. When can you be there?"

"I already turned around. Give me about five more minutes."

"Do you want something from Church's Chicken? My girl Teresa or LaMerle can probably hook us up," I said.

"Thanks. Get me a Cherry Coke and a two-piece with fries, please," she said.

"See you soon, baby."

As I approached Church's, I saw Daddy C in the parking lot arguing with a woman about three dollars. Daddy C was bandaged from head to toe and resting on crutches.

I pulled my cap over my eyes, buttoned and zipped my coat to the top, and approached the two of them. I did not recognize the woman. Even wearing a coat, she looked much too fragile and insignificant for Daddy C to be having an altercation with. I broke the two of them apart.

"What happened to you, sir?" I asked.

"I got shot, shit. One of them punk-ass youngsters got me the other night, 'bout three nights ago."

"At the Kat?"

"Yeah..."

I read about that this morning in the *Florida Times Union*. It mentioned two unidentified victims were rushed to the hospital. Now I know one of them. "I heard that them Gucci Brothers from Out East where responsible for that."

"Is that right?" Daddy C said.

"That's what I heard."

I turned my attention back to the argument.

"Sister, you are much too beautiful to be acting ugly in public. Here, take this and leave this man alone."

I gave her a twenty-dollar bill and handed my daddy a hundred dollars. He didn't even recognize me.

"Thank you, young man," she said and walked away.

"That's why he gave me more than you, bitch." He turned and shook my hand, then hugged me. "Thanks, li'l brother," he said.

I opened the door to the restaurant and smiled because I heard Daddy C say, "Now, that young man acts like he has some good home training; reminds me of myself back in the day."

I ran by Columbine Drive to re-up on a couple of packages that I kept hidden under a loose floorboard in Daddy C's bedroom. I made it to the Laundromat, book bag and chicken in tow, fifteen minutes after Jasmine was supposed to arrive. When I came around the corner, she smiled and motioned to her watch. I smiled and motioned to the food.

Jasmine opened the door of her Acura 3.5RL and gave me a small hug and a kiss on the cheek. She grabbed the food and asked me to drive. Jasmine said that she lived on the Northside, off Dunn Avenue, but I'd made different arrangements.

"First, I don't know how to drive. We never had a car for me to learn with."

Jasmine began to laugh. "I guess that's not funny, huh?" she said.

"I don't see the humor," I said.

"What's number two?"

"I need you to take me to The Adam's Mark Hotel."

Jasmine drove into the covered driveway of The Adam's Mark Hotel and I instructed her to park in the valet parking lane. The valet driver opened her door first, then mine.

"I guess you're paying him," she said.

"I'm paying for the room, you're paying for the parking," I said, without a hint of negotiation in my voice.

"What's up, Boss?" the valet driver said.

"All right now. This is Jasmine." I turned to Jasmine. "Jasmine this is Brad."

"Hello, Brad."

He waved hello.

I whispered to Brad, "Whatcha think?"

"Come on, my nigga, you're in the major leagues. You don't even have to ask me that anymore. They're all superstars. She's no different."

"Do you have the key ready for me?"

"It's right here. Make sure you introduce yourself to Rachel behind the desk."

"I will. Your package is in the Church's Chicken bag on the floor behind the passenger seat."

"How much time do I have? I might have to stop for gas," Brad said.

"I already checked the gauge; her tank is full."

"Good."

"But don't be stopping by to see any of your baby mamas." I leaned closer and put my arm around him. "Just drop the package, get my money, and wake me up at one-thirty."

"You just hatin' 'cause I'm having a long-ass senior skip day."

"Senior? Remember we left you in Ms. Washington's ninth grade English class."

Brad pushed me off him. "Who cares if I didn't finish? I'm rich now. I don't need no school."

I gave Brad a pound and handed him the keys to the car. "Drive safely."

Jasmine overstepped her boundaries. "What was all of that about?"

"What do you mean by that?" I said and waved her off.

I asked Jasmine to wait by the elevator while I said hello to Rachel. She asked to go to the restroom instead. That was even better.

"Hello. Are you Rachel?"

"Yes…and you are?"

"Boss–I mean January Calhoun, Brad's friend."

"Glad to meet you." Rachel retrieved a fax from the machine and skimmed it. I thought that she wasn't paying me any attention.

"Are those your real eyes?" she asked, without looking up.

"Yes, they are."

"Nice."

"Thanks."

"I have to get ready for a bunch of check-ins this afternoon; if you ever need anything, you don't have to go through Brad to get it. Here's my number."

Rachel began to hand me her business card, then retracted and scribbled something on the card.

"My cell phone number is on the back, if you need me for anything at all."

"Thanks."

"January, I'm ready," Jasmine said. She had put her hair up and looked better than she did at the hospital that morning. My guess is that she felt Rachel's Puerto Rican beauty to be some type of threat.

"I'll see you, Rachel."

Unencumbered by my grandmother's health problems or Daddy C's drama, riding the elevator upstairs, I was able to take a good look at Jasmine. At five-three, 115 pounds, and dipped in caramel, she was sexy. Her seductive but childlike tone of voice reminded me of Ms. Martinez.

We entered the hotel room, unsure as to why we were there. I kissed her on the cheek. "Thanks for picking me up."

"Do you respect me?" she asked.

"Of course, I do."

"I ask because I need you to know that this is not something I do."

"I feel you."

"I'm serious."

"How did I get lucky?" I asked.

"I don't know. Maybe you got game."

"As much as I'd like to believe that, you've known me for what, a few hours, and not consecutive at that, more like a few minutes. You don't know if I have game or not."

"I'm here, ain't I?"

Checkmate. I left it alone, choosing instead to give her a big hug. Her embrace was more comforting than plush five-star hotel bath towels or a mother's touch. I wanted to fall asleep in her arms.

I took my shoes and shirt off and pulled back the covers of the bed.

"Are you getting in?"

"What kind of woman do you think I am?"

"I'm going to sleep. I know you just clocked out from work, you're not tired?"

"Oh, I was fixin' to say..."

I didn't say a word and I didn't smile, but I wanted to laugh out loud because I knew if I wanted her, I could have had her.

We climbed in the bed together, and Jasmine rested her head on my shoulder. Her long jet-black, vitamin-enriched mane looked mismatched against the hundred plus nappy roots that sat atop my chest. The two types of hair clashed worse than old men wearing short pants and dark calf-length dress socks with white Reebok Classics.

Unable to fall off to sleep, we made beautiful intellectual intercourse. She enlightened and frightened me a bit in a biblical tirade on the subject of why *live* spelled backwards creates *evil*. We discussed teenage pregnancy and discrepancies in mandatory minimum drug offense sentencing guidelines and a few other social ills plaguing black America. I was aroused by the cerebral interaction, and though it was my policy to have sex with a young lady on the first meeting or cut her loose, I felt inclined to let this opportunity pass.

As is natural at this juncture of a "date," silence filled the room. I grabbed the remote control and turned to *SportsCenter*. Jasmine snatched the remote and turned off the television.

"Are you sure you want to watch TV *now*?" she asked.

"No, actually I want to take a nap."

"You want to take a nap *now*?"

My cell phone rang. Jasmine put it behind her back and didn't let me answer. When it stopped ringing, she placed it on top of the TV. I was too tired to retrieve it.

"What kind of person do you think I am? Why you think we came here? Let's go to sleep, man," I said.

Jasmine again laid her head on my shoulder. The warmth and size of her body felt good next to mine.

"Your girlfriend's a lucky lady."

"Shhh...go to sleep."

Brad called my cell phone at one-thirty to wake me, like I'd asked. Jasmine drove me back to the Laundromat, and Cindy drove her cousin's car the few blocks to pick me up. Study hall was our last "class" of the day, and we more or less supervised ourselves.

"I got bad news. Hurry up and get in," Cindy said.

"What is it?"

"I brought the roll for you to sign in, but you can't go back to school. JSO is looking for you."

"The police? Are they looking for me or for Daddy C?"

"It's for you."

I slumped into the seat.

"Okay...Okay...Give me the roll, let me sign that."

Cindy handed me a yellow legal sheet of paper. I signed it and selected a speed dial button on my cell phone.

"Hello, this is Seven."

"Hello, sweetheart. Don't say anything. I apologize for everything. I need your help right now."

"I already know. I overheard some officers talking about you at the diner this morning."

"Why didn't you call?"

"I did. Somebody answered, and I heard you saying that you wanted to go to sleep. I stayed on the line for a minute thinking you might pick up. I had to go to class after that."

"Anyway, I need you to take me to Lakeland. My girl Cindy will let Coach know what's up and take me to Jenkins Barbecue on Pearl Street. You can pick me up there."

"No problem. I'll get set now. You call me when you're ready."

"I appreciate it, baby." I folded my cell phone and looked Cindy in the eye.

"Okay…I need you to meet me in front of–I mean behind Old Pappy Johnson's house at three o'clock. I'll be sitting on an old Chevy Impala."

"Gotcha."

"But first go by Columbine Drive and tell Grandma or Daddy C if he's there, to let you in my room. Tell them you need my championship shoes for the game tonight. Look in the bottom right corner of my closet and grab one box of Dr. J Converse."

"You're going to play in those?"

"No. Listen. You carry the box downstairs. Don't let Daddy C go in that box. You'll find about twenty-five Gs in there. Grab two hundred dollars and buy me a new pair of something sweet in black–Nikes, size eleven, a

package of golf socks, and a pair of black wristbands."
What else? I thought.

"In the bathroom at the house, grab my toiletry
bag. Stop by Publix and grab me three or four oranges.
You can spend the change and bring me ten $100 bills
inside the left shoe. Hold the rest 'til I let you know
something."

I caught a ride with Calvin the Cabbie to my
Chevy and walked around the house twice in case someone
followed me to the car. I opened the door and laid face first
on the backseat.

CHAPTER NINE

March 6th

Dear Chevy,

It's me January. It's the first week of March, Friday. I have a surprise for you. Do you want the bad news or the good news first?

The Jacksonville Sheriff's Office has me in a Frank Abagnale, Jr. situation. I don't know what's going on, but word is that they're looking for me. But I'm like Frank; they'll have to catch me if they can.

I'll probably have to stay out of sight for a minute, until I can see what's going on. I won't be going anywhere near Durkeeville High. I stayed in school to play ball; I had enough credits last summer to graduate. I thought we had a chance to repeat in football, and I wanted to try and break Daddy C's scoring record in basketball. Well, both missions accomplished. The track team will have to make do with Earl Brown.

The surprise is that I'm going to introduce you to someone special. My friend Cindy is on her way here; I want you on your best behavior. After that we're going to Lakeland to bring home a state championship—in basketball. The boys and I have played together our whole lives, and God didn't bring us this far to drop us off here.

You won't believe it, but a part of me wants Daddy C to be in attendance tonight.   Love, January III

CHAPTER TEN

MY BROTHER, MY LOVER, MY FRIEND
By Seven Tennille
Student #JJFE4321
English Comp 2004
Dr. S. Madison

No, I don't have six siblings and my name doesn't have any special meaning. My mother named me Seven because her mother named her Six. It's not much different from Porsche's naming their daughters Mercedes or Lexus or fathers being Juniors christening their sons "III."

Being a poor country girl raised by two ornery aunts in a house with five cousins, one bathroom, and no males in sight, January is as much a father to me as I am a mother to him. I know that's one reason he picked me. All of his girlfriends or flings or whatever you want to call them, were older than he. He just doesn't know that's why I picked him.

I came to Jacksonville by way of Albany, Georgia. I wanted to attend Florida A&M, but my aunts thought that it was a party school so they sent me out here to Edward Waters College to study liberal arts.

When I first arrived, I lived with an uncle of mine who died five weeks and three days after he tried to rape me, which was four days after I got here. I was supposed to help him around the house in exchange for help with tuition, but he had bigger ideas.

One night at the downtown Jacksonville public library, this fine young brother walked in and asked to share a table with me. He noticed that I was reading *The Autobiography of Malcolm X* and commented on my choice of literature. He told me that his father made him read the same book when he was in the sixth grade. He also knew the poem "Invictus" by heart and dealt with all difficult situations by reciting the entire 23rd Psalm to himself. When the conversation turned to economics, both macro and personal, he seemed to have a calculator for a brain, and I was hooked.

He is younger than I, but much taller and more mature because of his experiences. We were made for each other, and I am not letting go of him, not now, not because of another woman, not ever.

I speak to January most every day, but I haven't seen him in a minute. I've been studying hard, trying to make January proud and my aunts envious. January is the most positive and motivating person who has ever been in my life. He believes that I can do anything-or at least that's the way he makes me feel.

He writes me these little poems or small verses, and they are precious. He would kill me if he knew I was telling you this, softening his reputation. I read them when I can't see his face.

Soft butter, pecan skin, and a soul that I miss,
whenever it's been more than ten minutes from her last kiss.
Curly auburn hair and soft, strong hands
that caress and underscore the distinction of wo-man from man.
The truth that brought us together is that I missed the bus,
Two of the "Tenth" eyeballing each other, deciding if it's more or
if it's just lust.
For reference, I contemplate using love, *but I continue to use* like,
looking at stars; half praying to God, talking 'bout I wish I may, I
wish I might.

January's life is not the easiest, and I don't agree with everything he is into, but I know he needs me. What kind of friend would I be if I couldn't love my brother?

I finished proofreading my writing assignment and turned it in to Dr. Madison. I asked for an excused absence, and he granted my request, adding that he wished my great-grandfather a speedy recovery (smile).

I rushed by Sam's Diner to pick up my paycheck. I wanted to be in place when January called. I pulled into the parking lot and looked up at the marquee. It read:

TODAY'S SPECIAL
FATBACK

I laughed. It reminded me of the country, which reminded me of Georgia, which reminded me of my aunts. My blood pressure rose, and a stress headache bombarded my forehead before I closed the door to my Honda.

I opened the door to the restaurant and those damn bells cranked up my headache a notch and ushered in an instant negative attitude. There were a large number of police officers gathered around the counter, and they all looked my way when I entered.

A few of them looked in Sam's direction. He glanced at me and lowered his head, nodding it in the affirmative.

"Sam, I stopped by to pick up my check."

"Like you need it," he mumbled.

"What did you say?"

The shortest and the cockiest of the officers dismounted his stool and approached me. "Hello, ma'am. Have you seen your boyfriend around?"

I rolled my eyes at Sam and faced the cop.

"To whom might you be referring?" I raised one finger for the officer to hold his thought. "And a glass of water, please, Sam."

The cop grabbed both sides of his holster and pulled it closer to his waist.

"One January Calhoun, III. We have reason to believe that you are dating him and may know where he is."

"If you're talking about the basketball player, everybody wishes they were dating him, sir. Look at your watch. Have you tried going by Durkeeville High?"

Sam handed me a glass of water and my paycheck. I stuck my tongue out at him.

"I see you're not going to be very cooperative."

I popped two pain relievers, washed them down with the water, and stood toe-to-toe with Officer Johnny Law.

"If you thought I was his girlfriend, did you really expect me to cooperate?"

CHAPTER ELEVEN

During the ten or eleven minutes that I'm high on crack-cocaine, I feel alert and confident. When I'm doing my first hit of the day, be it at 6:00 A.M. or 6:00 P.M., it is the rare time of the day that I think about anything unrelated to getting high. I spend those moments reflecting on the past and what shoulda, woulda, coulda.

I had a little money today, but bought me some ass and a carton of Newports. I gave the rest to Happy Jack, buying and drinking my last two beers about an hour ago, just as my psychological dependency on crack-cocaine kicked in. I've been on this corner, here at Eighth and Myrtle, begging for a few dollars to buy a rock every since.

I saw January, III earlier today. I let him think that I didn't recognize him. I can't believe he thinks that I don't know my own son when I see him. I'm a drug addict, not a blind man.

I can also see that I'm on the wrong corner. It shouldn't take a nigga like me a whole hour to raise ten dollars. I started to walk closer to the interstate, when I saw January's friend Trip driving by in a Nissan Altima. I noticed him not because he's Caucasian (white people buy most of the drugs in this area), but because of the damn rap music blasting out of a *white boy's* car.

I flagged him down.

"What's up, Mr. Calhoun? You going to the game?"

"What game?"

"The state championship. We're in it. Boss is gonna put on a show tonight."

"Where they playing–over at JU?"

"Jacksonville University…What you talking 'bout, Mr. Calhoun? The game is in Lakeland."

"I ain't got no way down there." I snapped closed three buttons on my orange Miami Dolphins windbreaker.

"I would take you, you know, but…well, look here Daddy C, I'm already running late. I missed the bus. See you next time."

Trip rolled up the window and turned up his music. I knocked on the window and motioned for him to let it down.

"Before you go, let me hold something," I asked.

"All I have are twenties."

"Well give me two of those. I'll let January know you hooked me up."

"I might not ever get my money back if that's the case."

I wanted the money, but I was also curious. "Why you say something like that?"

"JSO is looking for your son, sir. Tell him I said to be careful."

I jotted a mental note, but acted unconcerned.

"You still giving me the money?"

"Here, man. Whatever."

Trip handed me a few bills and sped away. In his haste, he gave me $60 dollars instead of the forty I'd asked for. I smiled and made my way to the crack house. "Hell on Earth" is what most of the addicts called it–address unknown, whereabouts kept secret.

We came and went without a fuss, ruining our lives on a residential block inhabited by decent welfare recipient poor and elderly people who tended to their own business and never, to my knowledge, questioned the motives of our presence. The large all brick two-story house where we abused the drugs was built in

1908 for a prominent Pullman porter and his three sisters. Although the house needed a fresh coat of paint and a way to insulate itself from rodents, the six bedrooms and solid oak wood floors hinted of a former estate, by turn-of-the-century other-side-of-the-tracks standards.

I paid the five-dollar entrance fee and bought a single $20 crack rock. At Hell on Earth, five dollars buys excellent service. Every room is prepared with your convenience in mind.

Next to a shade-covered lamp, laid on white handkerchiefs that themselves drape rickety metal tables, sat a pitcher of fresh, clean water, sterile glass pipes, and two cigarette lighters under an old poster depicting an egg frying in a pan with the slogan "This is your brain on drugs." The setup was like a package of cigarettes: neat and inviting with a "can't say I didn't warn you" Surgeon General's message in fine print. In one corner of the room sat two folded blankets and a pillow, with three packaged condoms resting on the arrangement like breath-mints; in another corner, stood a small trashcan.

I washed off my rock with the water then filled my pipe half-full with the same. I dropped the crack in the glass and ignited the lighter to heat it up. As the water began to bubble, the sodium bicarbonate made its usual cracking sound. *Ah the sound of mayhem at its infancy,* I thought.

When everything was right I inhaled the smoke. In ten seconds I was high as the ceiling, alert and confident. I basked in the euphoria for a few moments then decided to share my brain with my thoughts. At first, they ran to me faster than my heart pounded, then slowed to a crawl.

Why didn't my parents do something to help me when they found me drunk in the bathtub that Christmas? I was 10 years old. There was plenty of time to save me.

It is true, there's no such thing as bad children, just bad parents?

Can I be thankful for January and not be thankful for his tricking-ass mama? Can I be glad for the escape these narcotics allow me and hate the pain they cause? Drugs and alcohol are destroying entire communities.

My son and I are the poster children for what's good and bad in the hood. Damn! How did that happen?

The last time Durkeeville High won a state basketball championship I was hitting jump shots from the top of the key and only getting credit for 2 points. Back then dunking the ball excited the crowd sure enough, but it wasn't the end all that it is today. I could dunk with the best of them, but I preferred to finger roll and then slap the backboard with both hands. I was more of a passer than my son is, and I won more accolades doing it my way.

January did, however, inherit my killer crossover and jumping ability, which serves him well as the sport of basketball has come full circle as a game best played in the streets.

I be damned if I don't see him break somebody's ankles tonight.

I spent a full 10 minutes enjoying those few ideas. I know because I've done this ritual many times and because I was losing the high. That's it; times up–like a ride at Disney World the anticipation and the cost are much more than the actual event.

I broke open the bathroom door in search of the toilet. The adrenalin emptied my bowels every time I used crack whether I wanted it to or not. I cleaned myself, purchased a package of cocaine powder for the road, and left the building. I walked to the corner store and bought two quarts of beer. I rolled my change into a small cylinder, open on both ends, and ducked behind a Dumpster to waste twenty more dollars.

The serotonin and dopamine release hit me hard this time, and I ran into the street screaming for help. My hallucinations were much more vivid. Something was chasing me and getting closer by the second.

I took off my coat and my tie and threw them beside the road. I waved for somebody to stop, anybody. Driver after driver swerved out of my path and blew the horn or cussed me, or both.

The more they ignored me the more I felt the demon closing in on me. I had to leave town, and in a hurry. I needed to do something drastic to get someone's attention.

I removed the remainder of my clothing, leaving myself holding the beer and my nuts. At the same corner, I darted in and out of traffic, looking like The Juice rushing for yardage, still screaming for help.

The answer to my sick prayers came in the form of a Jacksonville Transportation Authority city bus. The driver pulled up to the stop and turned on his hazard lights. With no passengers on the bus, he was taking a break. He exited the bus and looked me in the eye, but didn't say anything. He picked a few pieces of lint off his uniform, patted his Afro, and walked across the street to the store.

I waited for him to enter the store and for the glass door to rest still. I pushed open the doors to the bus and placed my bag of beers in one of the front passenger seats. I scurried along the street, gathering my clothes, and threw them onto the bus.

"Hey, Daddy C, what are you doing?" somebody yelled.

I shifted the bus into drive and pulled away from the curb blowing the horn like a locomotive coming down the line. I drove up Myrtle Avenue, pressing the horn and waving at everybody I knew. My fellow drug abusers clapped and hollered. A few of them ran alongside the bus cheering. It was surreal.

I rode past Columbine Drive and looked for Sister Betty. As I figured, she was up sweeping the porch as I passed by. I took both hands off the wheel and blew her a big kiss. I didn't hear her, but I read her lips, *January–Oh my God.*

The driver left his cell phone on the bus and it rang several times, but I didn't answer. What was I to say?

I turned onto Eighth Street where this whole mess began and climbed up onto Interstate 95 heading south and away from the demons. I made it forty miles to Saint Augustine, Florida, before noticing that I was still butt-ass naked. I scooped up my shirt, slid my arms through the sleeves, opened the first quart of Budweiser, and drank a swallow. It wasn't ice cold, but beer at room temperature was enjoyable to me.

I was satisfied with the drink and satisfied with myself–the proudest I've been in a long time, I was en route to Lakeland– going to be a father to my son.

CHAPTER TWELVE

From a hundred yards away, the Jenkins Arena at Lakeland Center looks like a smaller version of the Georgia Dome in Atlanta. The surrounding landscape here is nicer though, benefiting from the central Floridian climate. And the fans get much louder inside than they ever did in Atlanta, pre-Michael Vick.

By the time we arrived, several yellow school buses already occupied the entire front two rows of parking. Teams representing the 1A and 3A classifications were also playing their championship games. We are 5A, meaning we have a student enrollment somewhere between eighteen hundred and twenty-four hundred, and the main event for the day. The other classes would play on the next day.

Two baldheaded black men wearing white sun visors, plain white T-shirts, and long denim shorts scalped tickets door-to-car-door.

"What's up, sister? Need tickets?" one of the men asked.

Seven lowered the window. "No thanks. I'm fine."

"That All-American out of Jacksonville, Boss Calhoun is playing tonight. You don't want to miss it…"

"I'm straight."

"How about you, young brother?"

"We have some passes coming, B, thanks." I turned my head away from the man.

"Roll up the window, Seven."

I began to unpeel one of the oranges Cindy bought for me. I tried to let negative thoughts fade and concentrate on the game. We haven't lost all season, although a team from New York gave us a scare in a Christmas tournament in South Carolina. I refused to let the losing begin tonight.

"Let's find a park or a playground or something," I said.

"We passed one, two exits back. I'll go there."

Seven moved her sunglasses from the top of her head back onto her pretty face and approached the street as if the whole world would stop and let her have the right of way.

"Seven, I appreciate everything you've done for me and I love you. You are more woman than I deserve." I placed an orange slice in my mouth.

"I would have had to go back home a long time ago if it weren't for you. No matter the money, I need you more than you know. Don't think that I'm trying to let you go."

"I don't want to complicate your life."

"Let me get something clear, January." Seven lifted the glasses onto her head and grabbed my hand. "I'm down for whatever."

I bit into another slice of the orange and nodded.

We exited the interstate at the same time as all seven of the Sixth Man Club buses passed us headed in the direction of the stadium.

"Did you see all those buses?" I asked.

"Where?"

I smiled. "Never mind."

"We need to talk to Dr. Mitchell," she said, changing the subject back to my immediate problem.

"I'm sure he knows. We need to talk to Jesus first."

"I already did. What are you waiting for?"

Seven pulled into the George Jenkins Recreational Facility, named after the Publix Grocery Stores chain founder. Several kids played basketball, and young mothers determined to stay in shape jogged through shrubbery-lined man-made paths.

The park was peaceful and innocent, the absolute opposite of my conscience. It was the perfect place to regain my composure. Seven challenged me to a game of HORSE.

She lost by one letter because I dunked the ball on my last shot. But again, she'd worked her charms; I was refreshed and at ease. We drove back to the arena and talked a security guard into letting me into the locker room before the rest of my team arrived. I assured him that I would not interfere with the other team's use of the room.

Seven went to rent a room at the Amerisuites hotel right there on the Lakeland Center property for the victory party and to watch the first half of the game on the local pay-per-view station. She would return with the getaway car to watch the second half of our game in person.

CHAPTER THIRTEEN

An audience of 7, 000 people doesn't seem gargantuan until they're yelling at once for you to go this way or that way, or telling you to do this or to do that. Dribbling up the floor, I looked into their eyes, searching for the right ones to bring me the magic that had escaped me for three quarters of the game.

I found it in a familiar pair. Seven didn't let me know that she was in the arena until two minutes had passed in the fourth quarter. I called for a timeout. Seven bounced down the steps to the sidelines. My teammates gathered around Coach H., while I stood on the outside of the huddle disgusted in my performance up to that point in the game.

She was holding my cell phone, which I'd wondered where it was and at that moment remembered that I'd placed in her purse while we were at the playground.

"Baby, you got to do better," she whispered in my ear.

I leaned forward and tugged on my shorts. "I'm trying."

"Daddy C called your phone and said that he's on the way to the game, but he's stuck in traffic near Disney World."

I stood silent.

"I hope you don't mind me answering your phone."

"He's trying to get here?" I asked.

"He's listening to the game on sports radio. Let's make him proud."

I didn't know what to think of the news. I wanted him at the game, but then again, I didn't.

"His team was the last Durkeeville team to win here," I said.

"I didn't know that." A big grin crept onto her face, and her eyes lit up the stadium, delivering the special ingredient I'd lacked all game.

"Have you heard anything I've said?" Coach H. yelled in my direction.

"No, sir. I apologize, but I'm ready now."

"Then show me," he said.

Earl passed the ball in. I threw it behind my back to Cindy's cousin, Dwayne, and cut hard to the basket. He lobbed it to me for my first dunk of the game and our first lead since halftime. That's all that our band needed to start the party. The Sixth Man Club, cheerleaders, and the rest of our loyal ghetto fans were up on their feet dancing as the other team called timeout.

The brass section of the band played and everyone else harmonized:

Bum…bu, bu, bu, bum…
Let's gooo.
Bum…bu, bu, bu, bum…
All riiight.
Bum…bu, bu, bu, bum…
Let's gooo.
Bum…bu, bu, bu, bum…
All riiight.

They needed more than a short pause in the action to stop me. I hadn't done much earlier in the game; I was ready to explode.

First, I intercepted a pass in the middle of the floor and raced to the basket alone. Instead of dunking the ball, I did a pretty finger roll and slapped the backboard with both hands in honor of Daddy C.

Earl stole the next one and threw it ahead to me to start the break. I let everybody run through the transition offensive sets then I buried a jumper from twenty -five feet for 3 points. Our opponents scored on their next possession, and I walked the ball up the court.

I was feeling good; it was time for a little entertainment. I dribbled up close to my defender and challenged him to take the ball from me.

"Just play ball," was his first response.

"We're on national TV, that's all you got?" I taunted, not knowing how far away the game was being broadcast, but doubting that people in Oregon cared anything about us.

"Come on, my nigga, try to take it," I said.

Sliding his feet, trying to keep up with me, he wanted to crack jokes.

"I screwed your mama last night."

I dribbled the ball back and forth behind my back.

"Maybe you did. I haven't seen her in years."

"Uh-huh, but I heard your daddy's a crack head," he said.

He asked for the trouble I was about to give him.

"You shouldn't have said that."

With his own cheerleaders crying for defense, he swiped for the ball across his body with his right hand. I gave him a hesitation dribble then crossed over to my left quicker than sand. Everyone in my earshot was laughing as I canned another three-pointer from behind the arc while that fool slipped and fell on his butt.

We were on a 10-2 run with no end in sight.

I was in a zone and I was angry. I'm not sure if I was mad because that boy called my daddy a crack head, or because of the fact that my daddy was a crack head.

Their point guard turned the ball over trying to break our press, and I walked the ball up again. I called for play number three and flashed a sign at Dwayne, running my hand past my throat. I dribbled around near the top of the key for a few seconds letting everybody run through the play. I made a sharp cut to my left as Dwayne set a pick a foot above the elbow. I set my defender up with a series of head and body fakes, then ran him square into Dwayne's broad shoulders. Dwayne added a thick forearm shot to the face for good measure. That boy never saw it coming and folded like paper. He had to leave the game because of bleeding. Dwayne picked him up as if he didn't mean to do it and the ref let him off the hook with a private talk by the far sideline.

But not before I stepped over the punk as he lay on the floor and said, "Whose head is cracked now?"

For that I received a technical foul. Coach took me out of the game and reprimanded me for my poor sportsmanship.

"He talked about my daddy, coach. What was I supposed to do?"

Ashamed of what I had done on the court and afraid of what was going to happen to me after I stepped off the court, I felt bad and wanted to cry. Agreeing to a police interrogation after the game in exchange for this opportunity was a big mistake. I'd never been this emotional and unsure of myself in my life, always able to look beyond the disappointments and the problems.

All the years of Daddy C humiliating me didn't mean jack. I knew he was on the way, but I needed a parent, a father, right now.

I didn't want my high school career to end like this. Leading by 10 points, I begged Coach to let me back in the game to make one more play.

Coach called for a timeout to put me back in the game. Everyone huddled around him.

"Okay, fellas. Boss brought us this far, let's let him end his career in style."

The team nodded in agreement and a few hands patted my back.

"We'll run Side-out. Earl Brown, you take out the ball and stay on this side of the court with everybody else; that'll draw your defender over to you to isolate Boss. Dwayne, you come from the opposite baseline and set a pick whenever Boss is ready, but don't hurt anybody this time. January…you do what you do."

Everybody gathered in closer and put their hands on top of one another's.

"I want to be able to tell me grandchildren about the year we went undefeated. We're at the door, let's kick it in," Coach said. " 'Durkeeville' on three–1… 2… 3…"

We replied in unison, "Durkeeville…a whoop!"

I caught the ball midway between the top of the key and half court. I glanced at the scoreboard and saw that there was 1 minute, 53 seconds remaining on the clock. Unlike the NBA, high school minutes are similar to real time, putting us in control of the game. I held the ball for a moment until my defender was forced by the rules to guard me. When he did, I went into my "And 1 Mixtape" dribbling exhibition. I bounced it between my legs and around my back. I crossed it over, back and forth, back and forth. I did a dribbling drill that forced the ball to bounce in a rhythmic pattern, and our band picked it up and played along to the beat.

The crowd loved it. I know it was a little flamboyant, but this was the last time in my life that I was certain I would be free to do what I wanted, and I did the Damn Thing.

The clock ticked to 1 minute, 14 seconds, and I got serious. I dashed toward the chump guarding me and made him commit. When he did, I used another crossover dribble to go by him to the right. For added assurance Dwayne came to the top of the key to set a pick. I rubbed off the pick, took one more dribble, two more steps, and jumped from the dotted line, holding the ball high in my right hand.

For me, time stood still for those four seconds I was in the air. Fans and the press took photographs. With each flash of a bulb I thought of a different person–first Daddy C, then Grandma, Cindy, Dr. Mitchell, Trip, and Seven.

I forced myself a little higher as I approached the basket. Using both hands, I slammed the ball through the basket with all my might. The ball hit the floor and bounced back up towards me. I caught it on my way back to Earth. Landing on both feet, I dropped the ball like a hot potato, and then stretched my arms wide and looked into the audience.

The crowd roared. I found Seven in the stands and winked. She blew a kiss.

I pulled my jersey out of my shorts and walked off the court and into the tunnel leading to the locker rooms under the deafening cheers of the fans of Durkeeville High, State Champions.

I looked across the arena for a last peek at Seven. She was up clapping and dancing like the rest of our fans. She looked spectacular in a pair of black Nine West boots, Express denim jeans, and coordinating Express blouse, but her intuition is her single most attractive quality. Her ability to make the correct decision at the right time is incredible.

The same security guard who let me into the Lakeland Center found me underneath the stadium and handed me a note. I asked him who gave it to him and he replied, "A cute little light-skinned girl driving a Honda Accord. She said to make sure you got this as soon as you came off the court."

"Thanks."

"I ran from the other side of the court when I saw you heading for the tunnel."

"Thanks."

"Good game tonight, son. You're better than your daddy was."

My daddy, I thought.

"Can I have your autograph? You know, for my son."

"I don't have a pen."

"Here's a Sharpee. Sign right here on your picture in the program."

I signed it:

WHAT WOULD YOU TRY TO ACCOMPLISH IF YOU THOUGHT IT WAS IMPOSSIBLE TO FAIL? KEEP HOLDING DOWN THE FORT, AND THANKS FOR EVERYTHING

JANUARY CALHOUN, III

He read it and said, "Thanks. That's perfect. Thanks." He patted me on the back as I walked away, unfolding the note.

January,

I knew y' all would win. Congratulations! Meet me in Room 715 next door at the Amerisuites.

When you exit the locker rooms, head due west, and you will find the stairways upstairs. Walk up to the fourth floor. There you will find a covered walkover to the hotel. The walkover is closed now, but only a small rope on both ends prevents people from using it. The good thing for us is that no one will be up there.

The guard who gave you this has the room key. Knock on the door before you enter.

Seven

    She always knows what to do, I thought.

    "Hey..." I called to the security guard. He rounded the corner, headed courtside. "Hey..."

    He heard me and backpedaled into view. I waved for him to come closer.

    "You forgot the key."

    "Oh, my bad, here it is." I said thanks and sprinted towards the stairwell. I followed Seven's directions and ended up in the hotel lobby.

CHAPTER FOURTEEN

I rode the elevator in peace, looking up at the ceiling. The doors of the elevator opened to the hum of vending machines and the sound of ice cubes forming that trailed me to Room 715.

I rapped on the door with my knuckles.

"Who is it?"

"Ah, it's January."

"Come in."

I slid the key in and opened the door, but did not see Seven.

"Seven?"

She walked into the living room. "How do you like this, Mr. MVP?"

Her pedicure was immaculate. Soft, muscular thighs supported the black satin nightgown that covered her ample breasts. It was the perfect material for her figure. Each inch of fabric grabbed or laid on her curves with precision. Her auburn-and-blond highlighted hair laid evenly on both sides of her face and down past her shoulders, bringing her spectacular eyes into view.

I believe she asked me to come closer, but I was mesmerized by her appearance. I did, however, hear her ask me to remove my shoes and leave them at the door.

After I did, she began to disrobe me, starting with my jersey. Her medium-length fingernails grazed my chest, sending chills down my spine. Seven untied the drawstring on my shorts, and pulled them off while looking into my eyes.

"You have gorgeous eyes," she said.

"You do, too," I managed.

My shorts dropped to the floor, and the rest of me stood hard as a rock. She helped me out of my jockstrap; not noticing the $1,000 taped to the inside, and led me by the hand across the thick carpet into the dining area, being very sure to use the satin gown and my rear view to her advantage.

The pathway to the dining area was covered in handpicked rose petals that tickled my toes. Votive beeswax candles flickered around the room, heightening the intimate atmosphere. A rich stereophonic sound of nineties hits, remixed as jazzed-out instrumentals, came from somewhere and filled the room.

In the center of the dinner table sat a vase overflowing with fresh colorful flowers. On the glass coffee table in the middle of the floor, I noticed a large silver-plated bucket filled with ice and two bottles of champagne.

Seven paused for a second. "You like?"

"Yes, I do."

We continued the journey; gliding across more rose petals into another candlelit room where I found a king-size bed blessed with satin sheets and sprinkled with baby powder. Against the wall was a large Jacuzzi brimming with what appeared to be milk. Milk?

Seven suggested that I brush my teeth and join her in the tub.

When I returned, she was naked and floating in the milk. She asked me to open the first bottle of champagne and pour each of us a glass. I did, and then another.

We laughed and joked about the game while Seven washed me with a men's fragrance soap she found at Bath and Body Works. I couldn't believe the milk bath. It was a new experience, and I must admit that it was silky and refreshing and left me feeling spoiled and pampered. But most of all, I felt sexual.

Seven stepped out of the Jacuzzi and asked me to hand her one of the towels next to my glass.

She didn't dry off; patting herself with the cloth, she left liquid droplets in places that made her body glisten under the candlelight. I swallowed another glass of champagne from the second bottle and stumbled out of the tub. My alcohol tolerance was non-existent because I didn't drink, and I rudely discovered myself drunk, nearly shattering my knee on the marble.

Seven dried me in the same manner she had herself. We stood there in suspended animation; from ten inches above I gazed into her eyes. Out of nervousness, I closed my left eye to wipe something away from it. When I opened it, Seven grabbed the back of my head with her left hand and my other head with her right hand and kissed me with a passion usually reserved for newlyweds or white children by the book lockers in school.

The combination of her large breasts pressed against my body and the gentle squeezing of her hands, came within five seconds of causing a problem for the rose petals beckoning us from below. She unlocked my mouth, and our eyes met.

Seven walked to the nightstand, pulled a condom from the second drawer, and drew back the covers on the bed. I motioned for her to climb in then crawled up the foot of the bed like a thief sneaking up on a Coach bag. Seven had turned me out up to this point; it was my turn to return the favor.

I grabbed her right leg and massaged the ball of her foot, licking between each toe. She squirmed at the mere thought of me sucking her toes. I looked into her eyes and put the big one in my mouth. Seven arched her back in delight. I moved from there to the insides of her thighs. I French-kissed both sides with long, exaggerated strokes, making sure to leave them sloppy wet. It was exciting to see her stomach muscles contracting.

There was a knock at the door.

"I forgot about room service," she said, moaning.

"I'll get it."

"No, January, I better get it."

"Well, you see who it is…then I'll get it," I said.

Seven skipped to the peephole and confirmed that it was room service. I wrapped a robe around me and answered the door.

"Is this Seven Tennille's room?"

"Yes, it is."

The waiter nodded. "I have room service for two."

He delivered a fine meal of king crab legs, lobster tails, steamed asparagus, and baked potatoes.

"It looks good."

"It does, but what's this?" I uncovered the last dish, which held the most appealing item of all.

Inside was a piece of hotel stationery folded in half and taped shut. I turned the note over. I looked at Seven for a suggestion, then slapped my palm three times with the piece of paper. The suspense was killing my high. I exhaled and opened it.

> *January,*
> *Look out the window.*
> *Daddy C*
> *904-751-5335*
> *I have your back*
> *.*

"Seven, go in the bedroom and look out the window and tell me what you see. Hurry up."

She ran to the window. After a few seconds, she called me into the room.

"Look out there," she said.

There were six police officers milling around three unmarked cars. They talked on cell phones and pointed in different directions. Hotel officials talked on two-way radios, I guess attempting to secure potential exits.

The note was written in Daddy C's chicken scratch, and I was willing to trust him. I didn't know the phone number he gave me, but I new the prefix to belong to Sprint Cellular and that it was a Jacksonville area code. I had to make a move fast.

"What's your plan?"

"Call Room Service and tell them the food is unacceptable. Tell them to send the same waiter back up here."

I rushed around the room putting back on my uniform. I ripped the money out of the jockstrap, leaving $100 aside. Seven stood still.

"Get ready, baby. I need your help, too."

I folded the other nine hundred dollars together and stuffed it into my left shoe.

Seven put on her street clothes and tossed me my cell phone.

"Thanks," I said. "You ready?"

Seven folded the collar of her jacket. "I must really love you."

The waiter knocked on the door, interrupting our Bonnie and Clyde moment.

"Is there a problem with the food?"

I yanked him into the room and put both locks on the door.

"Who gave you the note?"

"I don't want any trouble, young man."

I handed him the $100. "Was he wearing a suit, a nice suit? Where is he now?"

"In fact, he was wearing a nice three-button pinstriped number." The waiter held the bill up to the light to check its authenticity. "All I know is that he told me to give you the letter. He said to use the number on there to reach him."

"Okay. Take off your clothes."

"What the–"

I grabbed the waiter by the arm, and my eyes burned a hole through his courage. We both undressed, and I changed into his uniform. The shirt and tie fit fine, but I needed my Nikes to bridge the gap between land and water.

He directed us to the service elevator. Without an exact getaway planned Seven and I entered the elevator and called the number on the stationery.

"Hello. January?"

"Daddy C? What are you doing here?"

"Never mind that. Trip told me what's up."

"He did?"

"They think they got you surrounded, son–" *Son.* It sounded like Spanish coming from him–"but I'll get you out of here."

"We're on the service elevator on the west wing of the building...what's that?" I looked at Seven. "Hold on, Daddy C..."

The elevator slowed to a stop on the fifth floor, and we heard feet running. The doors opened and Trip was standing there. He looked me in the eye and prepared to flush twelve years of friendship down the toilet.

Trip looked down at his shoes. "I'm sorry," he said.

He backed away from the door and yelled, "There he is."

He should have run after that, but he approached the door and tried to drag me off the elevator. Seven jabbed the "door close" button again and again. I yanked my arm out of Trip's grasp and punched him in his big mouth. We saw him stumble into the arms of the uniformed officers as the elevator doors pressed together.

I was frantic. "Trip set me up, Daddy C," I yelled.

"Relax, son. Put Seven on the phone." Daddy C was calm and in control.

I handed her the phone.

"Yes, sir?"

"I will guide you to me." Seven looked at me and stroked the side of my face. "Get off on the third floor and take the guest elevator back to the fourth. Everybody is racing to the ground floor. They won't expect that."

Seven nodded and pressed for the elevator to stop on three.

"What are you doing?" I said. Seven waved me off.

"Then take the walkover back to Jenkins Arena. Take the stairwell to the second floor and exit the north gates of the stadium. That'll be the first set of glass doors you come to."

"Okay, then what?"

"Then start running!" Daddy C laughed. "The alarm will sound as soon as you open that door. I'll flash my headlights to let you know where I am."

"What are you driving?"

"Follow the flashing headlights."

Seven hung up the phone and stuffed it into her pocket. Pushing the service cart, I followed her lead. When we made it into Jenkins Arena, I ditched the cart and the tie and laced up my shoes.

"Why didn't you do that on the elevator?" Seven said.

I shrugged like the teenager that I am.

The alarm sounded, as Daddy C warned, and we sprinted in the direction of the flashing lights. As we got closer, two things caught my attention. One, that Seven beat me running to the headlights and two, that the outline of the vehicle surrounding those lights was too big for an automobile.

The sound of the engine shifting into gear confirmed my thoughts. Daddy C pulled the Jacksonville city bus into our path and opened the doors. Seven gave him a hug and spun into the passenger seat behind him.

I stood at the foot of the steps. "How did you get this?"

"Boy, get on the bus," he said and closed the doors behind me.

I gave him a pound. "Thanks, Daddy."

"Let's get the hell out of here."

Having eluded the police with Daddy C's getaway plan, we exited the parking lot without a fuss, and Daddy C merged onto Interstate 4, heading east. We traveled a full twenty miles without anyone saying a word.

Daddy C had been looking for a gas station in a desolate area and found one at Exit 321. He pulled into the station and slowed the bus.

"January, get out and see what side the tank is on."

I did and pointed to his right. The pressure of the gas pump was low, causing the gasoline to flow slowly through the hose, and we were all able to take a turn using the restroom by the time the tank filled. I went inside to pay and also bought a wine cooler for Seven, two quarts of beer for Daddy C, and a bottle of Gatorade for myself.

"Where y'all from?" the cashier asked, instead of saying "Can I see some ID for the alcohol?" or "Thank you, come again."

As we drove out of the station, the clerk picked up the telephone and looked in our direction.

"Daddy C, how did you know where we were?" Seven asked.

"The security guard you gave your note to is Jamal James; he played with us at Durkeeville High. He read your note."

"How did you find him?" I asked.

"I didn't. He saw me when I pulled the bus into the lot after the game." Daddy C drank close to half of the bottle of beer and laughed. "It's pretty hard to miss a Jacksonville city bus being driven in another town by a nigga looking good in a pinstripe suit– I should be a model for Ice Man and Mr. Kicks."

Seven and I laughed. "By the way, congratulations. I listened to the game on the radio."

Under the cover of darkness, we barreled on to Jacksonville. Watching the trees in the fields along the side of the road pass us as we went 70 mph, I counted the number of times Daddy C had been there for me when I needed him: When the principal at J. Russell called me a bookworm nigger, Daddy C forced his resignation *and* ambushed him leaving a PTA meeting, when Daddy C paid for me to attend a summer basketball camp following my eighth-grade year (where I first received national attention) after Coach reneged on his promise was the other, and then tonight.

As far as I was concerned, tonight was the one that Daddy C revealed the S on his chest. I didn't know how he acquired this bus, and I was certain that he was not supposed to have it, but he pulled a rabbit out of a hat for me.

He moved the brown bag away from his face and belched.

"Excuse you," I said.

"Excuse me. I thought you were asleep."

I carried Seven to a seat in the rear of the bus and rejoined Daddy C, trying to think of something to say as I walked up the aisle. He beat me to the punch.

"I've wasted so much of your time…so much of my own time."

"What I missed the most was your friendship," I said.

Daddy C looked at me through the rearview mirror.

"It's frightening by yourself, ain't it, being the only one around who gets it?" he said.

"You don't have anyone to share with." I looked back at him through the rearview mirror. "You spend all this time reading, studying...training yourself to be the best, and for what?"

"And if you're alone, you're probably lonely, too."

"That's what I'm saying," I said.

"But you're taught to strive to be the best." Daddy C looked into the side view mirror. "Who's teaching that shit?"

"People who just fit in, people who languish in the middle ground of the rubbish pile 'cause they would know better, they'd know it's not the purest place on Earth."

Daddy C swallowed a few more ounces of beer. "The fun is in the pursuit."

"No doubt..."

"Why you think all us, with all this talent, end up married to brown paper bags with glass-piped mistresses divorced from our potential?"

True enough, the country is filled with January Calhoun, Juniors. Men and women in every city capable of much more, but shackled by loneliness, low self-esteem, and drug abuse. *It won't happen to me,* raced through my mind.

"Can you hand me that other beer on the seat?"

"January, how did I get back here?" Seven stood and stretched. "Come here for a second, please."

I handed Daddy C the other beer and walked towards Seven.

"What's up?"

"Look out the window. I've been awake for a few minutes, and those three cars are our shadow. No matter who goes around us, or them, they've stayed right there."

I looked and recognized the cars to be Ford Crown Victorias–standard issue law enforcement vehicles.

CHAPTER FIFTEEN

The scrolling digital marquee advertising room rates at the Best Western International Drive, also flashed the temperature as fifty-eight degrees and the time as 1:18 A.M. Thirty-eight hotels sat stacked next to one another like $100,000 single-family homes in the newer subdivisions, separated from us only by guest parking spaces and thirty yards of weeds and grass. While most of the bright lights and billboards promoted the various theme parks, one set boasted helicopter rides for twenty bucks.

For the next seventeen miles through metropolitan Orlando, the scenery was much the same, interrupted by the downtown skyline, until darkness presided again outside of Sanford.

"January, come here, quick." Daddy C pointed to flashing blue-and-red lights about two miles ahead.

I ran through the bus, adrenaline beginning to rush.

"Yeah, they're behind us, too."

"You ain't no quitter, are you?" Daddy C looked me in the eye. "I know I ain't."

Daddy C gave me a pound and I had to have his back if I wanted to or not. But, I did have his back, and it felt good.

"Ain't no gas in it."

"Ain't no gas in it," he repeated. "I know that's right. Hold the wheel for a minute, son."

I reached across him and steadied the bus. Daddy C took a long drink of the beer, finishing it without coming up for air. He regained the reigns and opened the doors to the bus causing a strong current of wind to enter, pushing me against one of the rails.

Daddy C threw both bottles of beer into the road, one at a time.

As we approached the roadblock ahead, Daddy C pressed the pedal harder and hollered, "Hold on."

The undercover agents driving the three Crown Vics behind us blared their sirens as Daddy C pushed the bus over 90 mph. I looked out of the window at the beer cans and other trash on the shoulder of the road racing past us. Two of the three patrol cars in front of us formed a "V." The other was parked horizontally across parts of both lanes in the middle of the road. Laughing at the top of my lungs, I braced myself against a seat. Seven sat in the back and screamed.

With guns drawn, the officers crouched behind the vehicle in the second line of defense, anticipating the impact of the speeding bus.

Daddy C feigned that he was taking the bus on the right shoulder and then drove us right up the middle of their roadblock. He hit the front end of both patrol cars, bursting them into flames. We bounced off those and hit the third car square in the driver's side door and pushed it sixty feet before discarding it like an annoying insect by cutting sharp to the left and then hard to the right. The officers on foot scattered like cockroaches when a light is turned on.

The officers who'd trailed us for the last twenty-five minutes scrambled to rescue their fellow officers and cursed us from the other side of the inferno.

"Damn."

"What's wrong?" I said. "We made it."

"I blew out the left rear tire somehow," Daddy C said. "We need to ditch this thing. How far is it to Daytona?"

"About another twenty miles."

Daddy C continued driving, with us looking like we were on the topside of a big moving seesaw. Traveling at 60 mph we had a chance of making it to Daytona Beach before the cops closed in or the wheels on the bus collapsed.

Seven pulled on my shoulder.

"Are you okay?" I asked.

She grabbed onto me and did not let go. She had exhausted her bravery and her strength.

The headlights illuminated the fog surrounding the bus. Without any exits to advertise or highway changes or approaching cities to announce the state provided no road lights. The darkness hid the deer and any other potential obstacles.

The flashing hazard signals warned of our vehicle failure and symbolized the hopelessness of our condition. The lights from the speedometer, odometer, and such caused a glow around our faces, bringing into focus the fear in Daddy C's and Seven's eyes. I dared not look into the mirror to be proved of my own anxiety.

Like the calm before the storm, the three of us rode in silence as Interstate 4 merged onto I-95 North. The first exit, the one we chose, is the main drag of Daytona Beach, the same street fans flood on their way to witness the Daytona 500 NASCAR race. We resembled nothing of the sort passing by the raceway, thinking of what to do next.

International Speedway, as the boulevard is named, was unlike the last stretch of highway we covered. It was as bright as daylight.

"Let's get to the Greyhound station," I suggested.

"How far down?"

"Five or six miles."

We stopped at the traffic light on the corner of Nova and International Speedway. Daytona Beach has two malls, and to the left was the parking lot for one of them. To our right facing north on Nova sat one of Volusia County's finest. At first, the officer appeared to be reading some reports or something and then, sipping from a Styrofoam cup, he looked in our direction.

Our big broken-down, flashing, out-of-town city bus screamed for attention, but Seven and I stood statuesque, watching the cop's movement using our peripherals. Daddy C tried to look nonchalant, but rapped his fingers on the steering wheel and bounced his left leg liked he always did when he was nervous or having withdrawals.

"If we don't make it, I want you know that I tried," he said.

"We'll make it."

"But if we don't—"

"Move out. The light's green."

The bus rose from the pavement and crawled through the intersection. I guess it took the officer a second to digest the unlikelihood of the situation because he watched us go by without raising an eyebrow.

We exhaled prematurely. The officer turned on the flashing red and blue lights.

"Here he comes, Daddy C."

The officer cut off traffic, making a quick right turn to follow us.

"I'll let y'all out. Just walk away. Don't look back."

"What's your plan?"

"Don't know yet."

Daddy C drove us another two blocks then brought the bus to a stop, and Seven and I exited. The officer sped up to catch us. We walked in the officer's direction; Daddy C set still in the bus, no doubt planning his escape.

The officer talked to Seven and me through his loudspeaker. "Sir…ma'am, who else is on the bus? Don't move."

Seven grabbed my hand, but we didn't stop walking, and we didn't answer him. He pulled up to the curb about twenty yards behind the bus and got out of his patrol car.

"Hey! Come here."

I looked across my shoulder as he jogged to the other side of his vehicle. Daddy C jumped off the bus and screamed, startling the officer and Seven.

"There's your bus, Johnny Law!"

The officer tried to apprehend us by waving his finger in our direction as if he were our father promising us a good butt whipping whenever he caught up to us. He turned and sprinted towards Daddy. C.

Daddy C ducked and dodged his way up International Speedway, avoiding imaginary linebackers and free safeties, like we used to do imitating Emmitt Smith. The cop, Seven, and I followed, in that order.

Horns blew and people hollered as they drove, watching the action. The majority of the residents in the immediate area were black, many up this time of night sitting on their porches drinking beer or holding arguments. The chase brought a little unexpected excitement, and people began calling for the cop to leave Daddy C alone.

The mob grew by the second and they, too, joined the pursuit.

"Stop running!" The cop said.

"You stop running," Daddy C hollered back.

"I said stop running, nigger!"

Daddy C froze; stopped on a dime like Emmitt himself. Daddy C turned and walked straight towards the officer as the cop pointed his weapon at him. The mob rushed by Seven and me, bumping and pushing us out of their way. "Did he say *nigger*?" one of them asked.

The locals gathered around the cop. When Daddy C stepped within three feet of the officer the mob gathered closer.

The officer spoke in Daddy C's direction but looked around the crowd. "Put your hands up." He was nervous and unsure of himself.

My daddy raised his hands to surrender. The cop grabbed Daddy C's left wrist and then made the rookie mistake of placing his gun back in his holster.

Daddy C spun around and punched the officer hard in the face with his right hand. The cop swung back, missing. Daddy C hit him again, this time in the eye, knocking the cop to the ground. The mob rushed in, kicking and hitting the officer, screaming and cheering from a collective adrenaline rush.

The officer begged for the crowd to back away. The loud noises associated with the mini-riot smothered any pleas coming from anyone, least of all the officer. The locals seemed to enjoy their participation in what had quickly grown into an unnecessary violent nightmare, a Rodney King in reverse.

Trapped in a literal corner the officer pulled his gun and fired two shots into the air.

We all stood still. One in the mob gasped for air then hit the ground hard face first. The ground around him filled with blood, our hearts with fear.

"Look what you made me do!" The officer acted as if this was his first time shooting someone and even in self-defense was not proud of the outcome.

The cop scrambled to his feet and looked Daddy C in the eye. The mob dispersed, but the officer did not seem to care. The cop's lungs reached full capacity before exhaling each short, hard breath. The injured victim lay at his feet. Seven and I backpedaled away from the standoff. In the distance, sirens filled the air, later than sooner, as usual.

Daddy C looked at me, exhaled, and then raised both of his arms in surrender.

CHAPTER SIXTEEN

In the distance, lightning-filled clouds formed over Durkeeville, but bright sunlight ushered me into the lobby of The Adam's Mark Hotel downtown where botanical scenery and waxed marble floors provided instant serenity to my unraveling existence.

Spoiled trophy wives milled about the lobby talking on cell phones, rescheduling furniture delivery times and manicures. Conventioneers passed by in packs identifying themselves with loud HELLO MY NAME IS tags on their chests. Small-time entrepreneurs held private meetings over coffee and Cokes.

I stood holding several shopping bags, my temporary luggage. My cell phone rang, and I dropped everything.

"Hello."

"Hi, baby."

"How did it go?"

"I'm safe. The flight was a little bumpy, but short. There was a boot on my car. I had to pay eighty-five dollars to get it removed, but I'm on the road now. The coast is clear."

"Good. Spring break couldn't have come at a better time. Be safe, Seven."

"I love you."

"I know."

I gathered my luggage and approached the front desk. I didn't see Rachel, the Puerto Rican front desk manager, but wished I knew where she was; maybe she could hook me up with a room. It dawned on me to use her cell phone number, but that was in the garbage somewhere by now, since I left the clothes I was wearing the day she gave me the number in Lakeland. I turned to go ask Brad outside, but I stopped because I didn't want him prying.

"January…"

I turned back towards the front desk, and Rachel was standing there wiping the corners of her lovely mouth with a napkin.

"Where are you going?" she said.

I walked closer to the front desk. "I'm glad you're here."

"I saw you on the monitors in the back, but I was trying to finish my sandwich." She sighed and shivered as if to loose herself of anything unattractive. "When you headed towards the exit, I ran out here to catch you."

"Thanks. I'm happy to see you."

"How can I help you?"

I leaned closer to her and whispered, "I need a room for a couple of weeks." I rubbed the top of her hand and then squeezed it gently. "I have a li'l change, but I need to hold on to it for a minute."

She smiled and flirted with her eyes.

"Can you afford nineteen dollars a night?"

"Oh, yeah, that'd be real sweet. Do I have to pay up front?"

"I'd need one fifty-two ninety-five, including tax, now and the rest next week."

"Perfect. I'll have money by then."

I peeled off two $100 bills and handed them to her, being sure to let the fullness of my hand touch hers. After the new clothes and the $140 taxi ride from Daytona and the money for Seven's flight, I was left with sixty dollars.

My cell phone rang again.

"Excuse me a second, Rachel." I backed away from the desk. "Hello."

"January, it's Cindy." She cleared her throat. "Where have you been?"

"I'm around."

"You haven't been to school in a week, and Dr. Mitchell has postponed the celebration for the championship until someone can locate you. The whole school suspects the worst."

"Why they think that?"

Cindy didn't answer.

"Cindy, are you there?"

"Yes."

"Why do they think that?"

"There was a newspaper article about your daddy. It said he was arrested for grand theft auto, resisting arrest, DUI, inciting a riot, and some other stuff."

I heard her crying into the phone.

"Are you crying? Everything's all right, baby."

Cindy sniffled and blew her nose. "It said there was a fatal shooting during the arrest. Some people figured it must have been you, sticking up for Daddy C or something."

Rachel motioned for me to come to the desk. "Everything's ready."

I stuck one finger in the air.

"Don't cry, Cindy. I'm alive. I just have to lay low for a minute." I wiped my forehead and glanced at Rachel. She was

watching me and tried to look away when I looked in her direction.
"I'm glad you called. I need money."

"Good. I've been so paranoid carrying all of this cash around. Where are you? I'll bring it to you right now."

"Buy me a couple pair of cargo pants and stuff all the money in the different pockets. Then have everything gift-wrapped and leave the box in my name at the front desk of the Adam's Mark hotel. Give it to this Puerto Rican chick named Rachel."

"It's done. Can I let everybody know you're all right?"

"If I say no, is that really going to stop you?"

She laughed.

"Just don't let them know you spoke to me. Oh, and check on my grandmother for me, will you? Let her know I'm Okay."

"No problem."

"And Cindy…"

"Yes."

"Don't take this the wrong way, but…I love you."

"I know."

Rachel was on my side of the counter by then.

"Here are your keys, and here's your change." She handed me everything and placed her soft lips on my cheek. "It'll get better."

"Thanks."

She passed me another business card; with her cell phone number written on the back like the last one.

"You must have misplaced the first one because you never used it. Never make the same mistake once."

"Yes, ma'am. And here's something for you." I reached into one of my bags and handed her an orange.

She spun it around, tossed it in the air, caught it, and smiled.

"It's the least I could do."

"Brad told me about you and your oranges," she said.
"You trust me, huh?"

I made my way to the elevator and into Room 510. I dropped my bags in a corner and stared out of the window for a moment before closing the drapes. This was one time it would have been nice to have a close male friend–or at least a beer–but I didn't indulge in either. It was painful bearing these burdens alone. The good angel on my right shoulder urged me to open the Bible, but I resisted.

Instead, I called Earl to come pick me up.

CHAPTER SEVENTEEN

Big head Earl Brown arrived 30 minutes later.

"Where you want to go?" he asked.

"Let's go by the Kat."

"I don't have any money."

"Be for real."

"Will you buy me a beer, too, before we get there?"

"Sure. Whatever you want." I was in a laidback, stressed-out mood, both careless and careful. "But what kind of athlete drinks beer?"

He didn't answer, and I let him off the hook.

"Go down Fairfax, off the Twentieth Street Expressway. Turn left on West Twenty-fifth, and go across Spires to eighteen forty-five. They'll sell it to you in there."

When we arrived, I gave Earl my change from the hotel.

"Buy you a quart, and get all ones for the rest of this."

That one bottle blurred Earl's vision. It was, however, therapeutic for me to laugh at his reactions to the fine-ass girls arriving for work.

Cadillac after Acura after Navigator dropped off the various dancers reporting for the night shift as if they were chauffer-driven actresses on their way to a star-studded movie premiere.

We entered the building and the security guard frisked Earl. "Mama" was also at the door. Mama ran the place with skills learned in her native Thailand and on the streets of Miami.

"Boss, good to see you," Mama said. She motioned for the security guard not to put his hands on me. "I have something for you. Wait here."

"That's good. I need it."

"You know her?" Earl slurred.

"Long story," I said.

Mama was gone for five minutes. Patrons and dancers walked back and forth, in and out, the scenery improving my attitude by the minute.

"Here you are, my son," she said.

"If no for you, I have to close." Mama handed me an orange envelope and kissed my forehead, holding my face with both hands. "Fifty thousand now, more next time."

That is what she always gave me, and what she always said. She was a generous woman and knew how to repay a favor.

She patted Earl Brown on the arm. "This good son, right here; rich son, too. Give me loan two year ago. Business very good now."

Earl raised his eyebrows but said nothing.

"Hi, January," a dancer named White Chocolate said. She claimed to have a boyfriend in the Navy stationed at Mayport, out by the beach. Every time I ran into her, she said the boyfriend was out to sea. She'd whispered in my ear once that her mama had actually named her Nadine. I considered her a friend, a very sexy friend.

"Go now. Have fun," Mama said.

"Thanks, Mama."

In every strip club in America there's always one boisterous deejay behind the microphone, and the Kat was no different. We entered the inner chamber of the den of iniquity in time for his shout-outs.

"What's up, to all the fellas in the house?" he hollered over his music. "If you're just getting here, welcome to the world-famous Platinum Kitty Kat. I'm your host, Brother R. Love. If you've been here awhile and you're still begging, give another brother a chance..."

As background music, he spun a jazzy remix of Murder, Inc./Ashanti's "Always on Time." "Please, y'all don't forget to tip all this eye candy. Take a lick if you like, but you must break bread. These ladies are working hard for the money.

"Mike Fresh, I see you, boy... Ms. White Chocolate, I see you, girl... There goes my Uncle J. I see you, boy... Wait, I know them hoes ain't fighting over there... Security to the dressing room area, security to the dressing room." All ears where on Brother R. Love.

"There's the woman who pays the bills. Mamasan, those peaches and oranges on your dress are going off, I see you, girl... Look here, we have in the house tonight that nigga Boss Calhoun, I see you, boy... Oh shit! It's Earl Brown. What's happening? I see you, boy..."

Earl rounded up Nadine and three more of the best-looking dancers. The half dozen of us danced our way to the VIP section upstairs while the rest of the patrons looked on and mumbled. They didn't hate, they were there to conduct their own business. The Kat is the hustler's golf course.

We each selected our own personal dancer and the other two girls, more or less, rubbed our entire bodies, while we talked. I never was a big fan of nude dancing, but I was enjoying the head massage.

Earl had his woman doing some unmentionables, and I watched not knowing how to ask or even wanting mine to do the same.

"Boss, what happened after the game?" Earl asked.

"What do you want to know?"

"Where did you go?"

How should I answer this? I thought. Earl didn't give me a chance.

"I mean there is a lot of talk about you and drugs and women and your father. Hell, there's even a rumor that you own the Kat." He sat up a little. "I guess that one's true, huh?"

One of the girls informed Earl that it was her birthday and asked him for a gift.

"Don't you see we're talking? If you open your mouth to speak again while I'm in this building, you will be on the floor looking for your teeth."

She asked for that, I guess.

"It just doesn't feel right anymore," I said.

"What doesn't feel right?"

"My life. Man, I'm only seventeen years old! It's happening too fast, Cuz."

"You got a few things going on, huh?" Earl asked.

"There's a lot going on. Some of it, I don't even know what the deal is."

"I've got some serious problems of my own...like gambling. You know that, right?"

"Since elementary."

"I think I have something to deliver us out of all this gambling and drugs and what-not."

"I'm all for that." I thought about Seven. "I sure wouldn't want my girl to find out *what's really going on.*"

Earl motioned for me to hold my thought. "Okay, ladies, we appreciate all your help. White Chocolate, call down there to Jenkins Barbecue and order enough ribs and chicken for whoever is in the club right now. Tell 'em to mix the sauce." Earl looked at me. "Is that cool?"

I nodded. "You done placed the order now." I handed Nadine $600 for the food.

"No problem" and "Thanks, Boss" is all she said, with a devious grin on her face.

A chorus of "bye, guys" and the tapping of high heels accompanied the dancers through the hallway and down the steps.

"I need help. You need help, fine. So what's on your mind, Earl Brown?"

CHAPTER EIGHTEEN

It arrived two weeks after I purchased and moved into my new three-bedroom apartment, complete with flat screen plasma TV and 200-watt stereo on the lily-white Southside of town near Baymeadows Road.

The power of cash money is amazing. It makes most people overlook all the rules in this country.

I hadn't talked to Earl Brown in three weeks, and I hadn't seen the inside of Durkeeville High in five or six weeks. How it found me, I do not know.

The Young and the Restless was off and the gorgeous faces of *The Bold and the Beautiful* were flashing on the screen when the pounding on the door broke up my midday vacation.

As I entered the foyer, the doorknob rattled. Devoid of a peephole, I ran to the front window to see who was out there. An older white man dressed in a postman's uniform stood out front scratching under his arms. Out on the street was an official-looking U.S. Postal Service vehicle. Why was he trying to open the door?

I went back to the door and opened it without greeting. I grabbed the man by his shirt and jerked him into the apartment.

"Who are you?"

"Calm down. I have a letter for you."

"How did you get my address?"

"What?"

I tugged on his shirt tighter and closed the door behind him.

"Why were you trying to come in here?"

"I wasn't. It's a terrible habit of mine, turning people's doorknobs."

"Who's the letter addressed to?"

"January Calhoun. Is that you?"

I let go of his shirt, and he smoothed out his uniform.

"Yes, it is."

He handed me his clipboard. "Sign right here."

I did and the postman let himself out and rushed to his vehicle.

"And work on that habit," I said before the door closed in my face.

The envelope was regular letter size and white. My name and new address were handwritten in the middle and a preprinted return address with a blank space for a name was in the top left corner.

I grabbed the remote control, turned off the television, and walked to the island countertop in the kitchen. I flipped the letter over and back, then opened it.

Dear January,

Why haven't you come to visit me? Dumb question, huh? I'm writing in pen so I can't erase that. I'm doing all right though, if you care to know.

These jailhouse lawyers say that I may be looking at some real time, this time. The people at JTA are pretty upset about their bus, and the police officer in Daytona was off work for ten days with a broken nose and black eye. The district attorney seems to be coming up with new charges every day.

It may be what I need. What do you think? It would give me an opportunity to dry myself out. That's not to say that I can't get a drink in here if I want it. These brothers in here are geniuses–able to recycle the most unlikely items in the most unexpected ways. There's one cat who can make wine (they call it Buck) out of water and the fruits they give us for lunch. There's another who can "bake" a cake using those same fruits and the cornbread that nobody eats. Everybody uses orange and lemon peels as air freshener.

We talked about this recently, but this may be the one place where you can find other black men who "get it." The majority of black men in this country who are reading books are right in here with me or in other facilities like this. I guess that coincides with the fact that there are more black men in here or in other facilities like this, than there are in college.

In 1986 Congress enacted mandatory minimum sentencing laws that birthed a new holocaust. Apparently, they felt that more severe punishment would frighten the crime out of criminals, but the penalties and these facilities don't deter crime, they beget crime. Instead of curtailing criminal tendencies, violent behavior is fostered. Not only are these places costly to American taxpayers, their only tangible accomplishment is the overcrowding and agitation of nonviolent offenders until they become violent ones.

However, if you don't have to waste your time defending your life, you can develop it. With nothing but time on your hands, this is a great place to expand your mind. I see how Malcolm found Allah and learned both the Holy Bible and the Holy Koran in here. I understand how Martin could have crafted his "Letter from a Birmingham Jail" in a place like this.

The sad truth is that there is a wealth of black gold behind these bars, wasted talent in a jar–a collection of individuals underachieving on the streets turned scholar in the belly of the beast. I would bet that the intelligence was always within, but the knowledge was tucked away in a book.

Jesus or Allah must live within these walls. How else could a man be motivated to improve himself under such harsh conditions, when he wouldn't do it on the streets where he was free, where admission to church was free, where a library card was free?

Son, find Jesus before He finds you. Forget about what we said and continue to strive to be the best. This is not where you want to end up. I am not how you want to end up. Do as I say, not as I do.

You know that once upon a time, I sat where you sit. You have your life before you. Understand that and cherish the idea. Don't make decisions that have consequences you don't want to endure.

Think about it. If I could find you, don't you think JSO could, too, if they wanted? Even in the terrible shape I'm in, my hands still reach far and wide. I will cover you for as long as I can, then you will have to decide for yourself, what's best for you.

When I called, your grandma reminded me of something: we all learn as we go along. Everyday learn something new. I have always loved you. Now I'm learning to love myself again.

Go see your grandma. I gave her your address. Write me back before I go to court. There won't be much of a trial; they caught me red-handed with plenty of witnesses. Let me know what's up with your scholarship offers. How's that cute girlfriend of yours?

                    I love you,
                    January Calhoun, Jr.
                    Daddy C

My daddy didn't speak to me with such eloquence. Other than in passing, he didn't speak to me very much at all. Our escapade after the championship game had done some good. Maybe Daddy C's incarceration would do more.

His words blew me away, so I decided to read the letter a second time. Before I did, I grabbed a dish from the dishwasher and scooped myself a large bowl of ice cream–chocolate mixed with vanilla, the way Daddy C would have done it.

CHAPTER NINETEEN

I never trusted the taste of strawberry ice cream, so it sat alone in the kitchen sink, melted away in an otherwise empty box of Neapolitan.

Big heavy raindrops escorted sunrise and the first day of spring break for Duval County schools. Gumball-size hailstones pounded on the new pearl-black Escalade Jasmine rented for me to drive for the weekend.

I watched from the kitchen window of my apartment as the frozen rain wreaked havoc for all of thirty seconds then slowed to a drizzle, wishing that I could rent a set of rims for the internally luxurious, yet externally ordinary truck parked outside.

The Black College Reunion in Daytona Beach started on the same day and expected a huge crowd, rain or shine. I planned to be in that number. I scrambled eggs and oven-fried smoked turkey sausage to the tunes of Pharrell Williams and Chad Hugo. I didn't have much of a musical choice–their tracks dominated the radio airwaves.

My cell phone rang and then stopped after two rings. I looked at the caller ID and saw that it was Earl's number, and decided against calling him back.

On the drive home from the Black College Reunion, I watched sixty-five minutes of video footage through my digital camcorder LCD display while steering with my left knee and rewinding the outrageous scenes with my right hand.

There was a shot of a few homeboys from Durkeeville hollering out of their car window at me. There were several shots of good-looking college women singing into the camera, "Hi, January," as I had asked them to do. There was tape of professional football players and other celebrities in my hotel suite Saturday night. I shook my head thinking about how that happened and rewound the tape to that segment.

A few Jacksonville Jaguar players, knowing me only from the Jacksonville daily paper, were in Daytona and asked if I wanted to hang out with them. I accepted their invitation and was given a beautiful honey to mingle with, tossed to me like a screen pass out in the flat.

Later, the group of us went to a concert and ate Buffalo wings and drank bottled water backstage like entertainment-business moguls–or groupies, depending on how you want to look at it. I didn't see much of the show, I watched my date Erica's ass jiggle and breasts bounce while she screamed at whoever was on stage.

After the show, Erica asked if we could go back to my room, and that's how the whole group of them ended up at The Adam's Mark Hotel *with me.*

My recollection and my imagination entertained me the rest of the trip. After refueling the Escalade at the Gate gas station on Busch Drive, I continued to Jacksonville International Airport where I was to return the rental car and await Jasmine's arrival.

The rental return agent approached the car as I collected my bags.

"Hello, sir. Did you enjoy the car?" She didn't wait for a response as I handed her the rental agreement.

"Will you be leaving this on your credit card?"

I'd wanted to pay cash, but decided that I would pay back Jasmine later.

"Yes."

"Here you are, sir. Thanks and come again." She tore off the receipt and hurried to another car.

I walked to the area outside of baggage claim and leaned against a pillar. Out of the corner of my eye, I noticed two uniformed police officers looking in my direction. They made me feel uneasy, and I moved to the other side of the pillar. After a few seconds, I stretched out my arms to play it off and peered across my shoulder to check their position…and they were gone.

I breathed a sigh of relief and looked in the other direction. I felt a gentle hand touching my right shoulder and a firm masculine hand grabbing my left. I was disoriented and quickly looked left then right, surprised to see the owners of both hands.

"Hi, baby" and "Are you January Calhoun?" came from opposite directions and registered in my head at the same time.

"Ah…hold on, officers." I looked towards my baby. "Seven, what are you doing here?"

"Mr. Calhoun?"

"I followed you from the Gate station. You were in your own little world."

I squeezed her hands and turned back around.

"Yes, officers, how can I help you?"

"Are you the same January Calhoun with Durkeeville High?

"Yes, sir, I am."

"Is everything all right, January?" Seven asked.

"We just want your autograph, son. My wife thinks you are the next Michael Jordan." He smiled.

"And can you sign one for my son, too. I think he is your biggest fan," the other officer said.

They both offered their JSO issued notepads and a pen. I thanked Jesus under my breath and obliged.

"Thanks, Boss. Ain't that what they call you?" The taller officer said.

"Yes, sir, you're welcome."

The other officer tipped his ball cap and smiled.

"No problem." I looked at Seven's angelic face and again thanked Jesus under my breath. "Is there no help for the widow's son?"

"I'll give you a ride. Come on."

We started across the walkway to the garage.

I love to watch Seven move across the Earth. I'd spent the last 60 hours surrounded by half-naked women and none of them were as sexy as Seven with her clothes on.

I hadn't seen her in jeans in some time, and I found it arousing to see her luscious backside supported by those toned semi-bowed legs. Perfectly elevated breasts, accented by a platinum navel ring-bejeweled six-pack, supported a cute long-sleeved blouse made of some type of thin stretchable material.

The shirt was nice. The design on it featured about twenty wallet-sized pictures of a smiling little black boy sporting an Afro. Scribbled on the back was a quote that I recognized as one of Dr. Martin Luther King, Jr's: "*Sooner or later all the people of the world will have to discover a way to live together in peace.*"

"Who were you waiting on?" she said.

"Who was I waiting on?" I said, stalling for time. "What do you mean?" I was still shook from the episode with the policemen and her seductive walk. I was not expecting Seven to say that.

"Hey, January, where are you going?" a familiar voice yelled.

Jasmine turn around and get the hell out of here is what went through my head.

Now, Seven knew the answer to her question and did not hide her emotions.

"Is that bitch calling *you*?"

"I don't think so. Where's your car?"

"January, over here!" I guess Jasmine was not going down without a fight.

I looked across the driveway and pretended to search for the origin of the voice.

"I don't see anybody. Let's go."

"She's right there. What are you doing at the airport anyway? I thought you went to Daytona Beach."

"I did."

"Did you fly? Or were you here picking up that bitch?"

"Why would I have my luggage if I was picking her up?"

"Oh, so she's picking you up?" Seven raised her hand like a human stop sign and shook her head. "Oh, so she rented you that Escalade, and she's here to pick you up."

"Baby, I don't know what you're talking about."

While my back was turned, Jasmine had made it across the walkway and was within ten feet of us.

"Listen, you...you mother...hey...don't call me anymore and forget about sexing me anymore. I thought you was all this and that. You just like the rest of 'em." Jasmine threw the first thing she could find, which was a fistful of sand, and stormed off.

I threw up my arms and ducked as most of the sand landed against my back and in my hair.

Seven stood with her arms folded, tapping her foot.

I stood looking like a very young old man.

"Baby, I don't know her. I never had sex with her." I offered a halfway honest explanation. "You know how people can be, after a game and all that, you know, stalking me and stuff."

Seven turned and walked off.

"You still giving me a ride?"

She kept walking, but that was better than a no. I brushed myself off and ran after her. She let me in the car, but didn't say a word during the drive home. I gave her directions to my new apartment and shut up. She rolled her eyes at me and blasted the volume on her stereo.

CHAPTER TWENTY

Once we were inside the gate to my apartment community, Seven stopped the car and I collected my mail. Along with a few bills and coupons to Pizza Hut, there were two other pieces of mail.

The first was a large tan envelope from Grandma. Inside was a full sheet of paper with only 1326 COLUMBINE DRIVE and 399-1968… IN CASE YOU HAVE FORGOTTEN written on it, three letters from Florida A&M, and one letter apiece from Duke, Memphis, and the University of Florida. There was also a crisp clean white envelope, the size of a birthday card, adorned with remarkable penmanship, unburdened by a return address, but postmarked in Jacksonville.

Seven and I entered my apartment without speaking. My thoughts were on the mail and apparent from her negative body language, her mind was still at the airport. I closed the door behind her and watched as she took a quick look around.

"Nice place."

"Thanks."

"Did you decorate it all by yourself…or did she help you?" Seven removed her purse from her shoulder and slung it onto the sofa as she sat down.

"That's it, baby! Nobody helped me do anything. And I'm not gonna be going on and on about this same old shit."

Seven rolled her eyes.

"I apologize for whatever happened. But that's it on that. I want you to stay, but if you want to go–"

"Did you sleep with her?"

"No. I did not sleep with her."

Seven ran her index finger across the sofa, around and around, in a figure eight. I moved towards her and sat on the sofa two feet away from her outstretched hand. She looked up into my eyes then down at her invisible drawing.

"I'm not going to class tomorrow. Can I spend the night?" she said.

"No problem. Why don't you take a shower? You can put on one of my T-shirts."

We both stood, and I hugged her with my heart. She didn't let go of me until I let go of her, and I loved her even more for that.

When I heard the water running in the bathroom I rushed to open my mail. Grandma's note made feel ashamed, but it was humorous still.

The letters from the three Division 1-A schools said the same thing: We want you, but where the hell are you? Duke and Memphis withdrew their offers and Florida said that if this kid from Orlando signed first, they wouldn't have room for me. These letters were postmarked between nine and fourteen days earlier, respectively. You win some, you lose some was the position I decided to take. I'd saved my money for this very day, so I'd have money to attend college.

Florida A&M University employed a more subtle approach in that they asked for me to let them know if they could help me in any way. They also offered to let me play quarterback and play basketball...and sign whenever I was ready.

Wow, I thought. I think they didn't feel they had a chance anyway—why not offer me the moon?

The last letter was from the president of Florida A&M offering a full four-year *academic* scholarship. I had never heard of such a thing.

I studied the handwriting on the greeting card-sized envelope. The letters were small and cute, drawn with absolute clarity. Their perfection seemed possible only by computerization. The words were not written in cursive, but the elegance of each letter flowed effortlessly from one to the next, as if they were. I knew a Korean girl in seventh grade, Hoa Pham, whose printing was as beautiful, but couldn't fathom why she would be writing me.

And of course, she wasn't. I opened the envelope and found a strange but interesting greeting card. On the cover was a bright four-color process print of a black woman in her mid-twenties, knees bent with her arms outstretched eagerly anticipating the embrace of the young black boy running towards her. The inside of the card was blank except for these words:

We stand tall, boldly challenging Death every day. But as soon as he arrives we crumple up, folded like paper, crying ourselves to sleep. Death is cold, yet calming. Death is omega, yet alpha. But most of all Death is inevitable and everlasting.

The Bible teaches us that the wages of sin is death. Therefore, we all solidified our positions in the ever-after many years ago, even before we knew so. Why then do we suffer so much when loved ones are called to pay the fiddler?

More than likely guilt and fear top the list. We fear that we didn't honor the recently expired life in the best way that we could have. We feel guilt for not living our own lives more abundantly. We finally realize that tomorrow is not promised, and it frightens us. We are sick to our stomachs because we didn't respect the past and we are not celebrating the present. Many of us live in constant struggle and unpleased. We fight so hard to make things go our way and sadly miss the things that come our way; never truly surrendering to the fact that God does want us all to be happy, healthy, prosperous, and at peace.

The unfortunate part is that we won't get a second chance at life on Earth. Therefore, take advantage of the life you have, the time you have been given. Learn to live life on purpose, not by accident. We must decide that we are going to be happy while we can, no matter what. We must learn how to take life's lemons and turn them into lemonade. It may not be a perfect life or exactly the life you planned, but it can be fruitful and tremendous.

I Love You,
Mama

Mama? What kind of joke was this? It wasn't very funny. If my mama did send me this, why didn't she include a phone number or an address? How did she find me? I wasn't sure she was even alive.

Knots formed in my throat and pockets of tears formed in the corners of my eyes. My mouth trembled like an eight-year-old's after a terrifying spanking. I took a deep breath, trying to suck back in my emotions.

I walked circles around the sofa trying to make sense of the message. I needed a friend; I needed a hug.

I trotted and skipped down the hallway to the bathroom and burst through the door.

"Seven."

She pulled back the shower curtain. The water bouncing off her body, and the naturalness of her wet hair resting on her back provided the tenderness I was seeking.

When she said, "What's wrong, January?" I let it go. I dropped the card and climbed into the shower with Seven, crying like a baby.

I hugged her and tried to relax.

"What's wrong?"

Seven stroked my chin a few times and wiped at my eyes. I looked up at her, and she kissed me on the cheek. She decided to stop asking me questions and held me until my clothes were drenched and sticking to my body.

Seven turned off the water, and I removed my clothes to dry off. She waited for me to speak. I didn't open my mouth until we were lying on the floor in the living room.

"I got a letter from my mama, today…I think."

"Is that why you cried?"

"Yeah, because first of all, I didn't even know that she was alive."

Seven rubbed me on my thigh.

"Then, I don't know if somebody is playing with me or what."

"I understand."

"Plus, it was a beautiful card, but it was about death and dying. Was she trying to tell me something?"

"Let me see the card."

I went and picked it up off the floor and brought it back to Seven.

"This is perfect handwriting," she said.

"That's the first thing I noticed, too."

Seven read the card then placed it on the coffee table, away from the magazines. She walked to the window, pulled the curtains apart slightly, and looked out. The moonlight was her friend.

"When is the last time you heard from her?"

"I was like nine years old." I walked to the window and held Seven from behind, our towels separating our naked bodies.

"If she's trying to tell you something, do you want to know what it is?"

"Should I?"

Seven turned and kissed me on the cheek. "You need to talk to Daddy C."

"I was hoping you wouldn't say that."

CHAPTER TWENTY-ONE

Inmates housed at the John E. Goode Pre-Trail Detention Facility with last names beginning with the letters A-C are allowed visitors on Mondays and Saturdays. I was bewildered by the mysterious greeting card, caught up in the moment, and almost made a disastrous mistake in going to visit Daddy C on that Monday after reading the card.

I slowed down, caught my breath, and realized that visiting him was not in my best interest. Instead I laid low and spent the week reading *True to the Game* by Teri Woods and *Men Cry in The Dark* by Michael Baisden. I caught a taxi to see Grandma on Saturday.

Durkeeville was in full effect at 1:30 P.M. A rainbow of beautiful shades of black moved about with pride and a sense of direction like their predecessors in 1920's Harlem. The canvas was painted in more of a hip-hop hue, but having spent the last several weeks on the melanin challenged Southside, it was a sight for my sore eyes, yes indeed.

The heat index was above 90, due to the humidity. Sirens filled the air, the sound coming from all directions like ghetto bass. The Ice Cream Man's truck was parked on the corner and surrounded by kids on Big Wheels, grandfathers leaning on walking canes, and all in between. Bubble Chevys on Dayton rims and $60,000 SUVs raced up and down the narrow streets like country boys on back roads.

A fine-bodied gold-toothed prostitute worked the corner in broad daylight.

"Hey, baby. You want some head?" she asked as I stepped out of the car.

I paid Calvin the Cabbie. "Things sure haven't changed," I mumbled.

I approached 1326 Columbine Drive with the nervousness of a runaway child, hoping to return to love that wasn't evident in the first place, praying that punishment for the disappearing act did not wait on the other side of the door.

The neighborhood kids screaming my name and tugging on my Julius Erving New Jersey Nets throwback nearly spoiled my surprise. I motioned for them to calm down and be quiet, passing out two dollars apiece to all who respected my wishes.

I knocked on the screen door, making more noise than necessary.

My unintentional pounding of the door didn't rival the tongue-lashing going on inside the house. Grandma was talking to another woman. I knelt down and moved closer to the door.

"I told you, I don't think it's a good idea," Grandma said.

"So what'll happen when I'm dead and gone?"

"You got a lot of nerve. You ain't been around all this time."

"What I mean is—"

"Woman, to us you already dead."

"You don't mean that."

"God forgive me, but you gon' make me slap the mess outta you!" Grandma said.

The unidentified woman started to cry. I didn't recognize her voice and didn't know what she could have done to get on my grandmother's bad side. I had never heard Grandma speak in such a forceful tone. I reasoned that old girl must have deserved it.

"Those tears will get you nowhere."

Quick, hard footsteps raced towards me. I tried to straighten up, but was too slow. The front door swung inward, allowing a gush of wind to knock picture frames and small plants to the floor. The screen door burst open, the metal frames rattling and shaking, hitting me hard on my left ankle, forcing me back down on the floor of the front porch.

I rolled 360 degrees and came to rest on my back. From my bird's-eye view I watched the crying woman go by. Milliseconds turned into minutes. The woman looked to her left, and we made eye contact. Her eyes were hazel and almond shaped, her eyelashes thick, eyebrows arched and pencil outlined. Her full lips opened revealing straight white teeth that allowed the words EXCUSE ME to pass through.

She stood about 5'9''. She was a little overweight, even for her height, but her choice of tight-fitting jeans and semi-unbuttoned cotton blouse revealed the body of a former swimsuit model.

She bounded down the steps of the porch to the sidewalk. Grandma followed, Bethune-Cookman College T-shirt hanging low on her gray sweatpants, cursing underneath her breath.

"Grandma, what's going on?" I uttered.

"January...what are you doing here?"

The woman turned and moved towards the porch. "Is that you, January?" she said.

"Get off my property," Grandma yelled.

I crawled to my feet. The woman retreated as Grandma marched out into the front lawn. Only twelve feet of grass and sidewalk separated the porch from the street. One of the woman's three-inch heels became wedged in one of the many uneven cracks in the sidewalk. Off balance, her arms flailed from side to side.

"Can you help me, please?" she asked of no one in particular.

One of the two small girls hosting an imaginary tea party on the sidewalk tried to help her out of the crack while the other laughed.

I looked to my right and heard bass pounding from 15" woofers and getting louder by the second. A pearl-white Cadillac CTS with shiny 20" chrome rims rounded the curb, appearing from behind the ice cream truck out of thin air. A candy apple-red Ford F-150 with identical rims followed, closer than the law allows.

My old friend Trip was driving the Caddy. Instead of watching where he was driving, he looked out of his window to the driver of the second vehicle. A dread-headed dark-skinned brother was driving the second truck and pointed in my direction. Trip turned and looked at me and stared as if he'd seen a ghost.

The woman yanked her heel out of the sidewalk and stumbled backwards into the street, passing between two cars parked on the curb.

Everything sped up, faster than real time–if that's possible.

Tires screeched and burned up the pavement, causing a large cloud of smoke. The beats coming from the Caddy, the Ford, and the ice cream truck blended seamlessly together with the little girls' laughter and the birds chirping and my heart pounding and Grandma quoting Scriptures and lizards running through the grass and squirrels climbing through the shrubbery to create a theatrical score that ended in one big crescendo of cymbals crashing together as Trip's Caddy slammed into...

"My baby!" Grandma cried out.

The bones in the woman's body cracked loudly, the same as when children foolishly pop their knuckles. Her body elevated from the pavement and hurled into the windshield. The brown Coach bag she was carrying flew into the air fifty feet and landed behind me as I ran to Grandma's side. I tried to hold my grandmother, but she was hysterical, her outburst too powerful for my embrace.

"My baby! My baby!" played again and again in my mind as Grandma continued to yell out the same. I brought Sister Betty to her knees and retreated to examine the purse.

I let the confusion around me entertain itself. My subconscious revealed the missing link, but I was not quick to receive it. I had to open the bag for myself and let the truth clarify any misunderstandings.

The purse was new, the price tag still hung from the shoulder strap. The leather inside the purse smelled fresh. Unencumbered by many belongings, except for a matching wallet, a bottle of Ralph Lauren, and a small pack of Kleenex tissue, the bag was bare. I opened the wallet to find $500, a library card, and a picture... of me. *I knew it! I knew it! I knew it.* The driver's license displayed a picture of the same woman resting across Trip's windshield, with the same name as my mama's–Druscilla Thelma Calhoun.

The address was unimportant to me and so was the age, because neither mattered anymore.

The dread-headed boy jerked the Ford F-150 into reverse and sped away. The growing crowd of spectators and cars parked alongside the curb trapped Trip. He was disoriented from the impact and the sheer horror of the collision. He bled from the mouth and the forehead, the airbag having discharged and kicked his ass.

But it was nothing compared to the beating I was about to give him.

I dragged him from the Caddy and body slammed him on the hard pavement. I kicked him twice and began to cry. I bent down and punched him unconscious. Blood flew from his face and splattered on the rims.

"That's for all the backstabbing."

I hit him again, this time swinging from left field.

"And that's for my mama."

Cindy, my guardian angel, appeared and pulled me off Trip. She looked bad. Her face was still cute, but she'd lost close to twenty-five pounds.

"Don't you hear those sirens? Get out of here," she said.

I grabbed both sides of my head and tried to shake some sense back into it.

"Thanks, Cindy." I bolted down the street, jersey flapping in the wind, and disappeared from the scene.

I caught the city bus home and hid out in my apartment. I paced back and forth, wanting to go back to Durkeeville and check on Grandma. I flicked on the TV hoping to catch an Action Newsbreak, but it never came.

I didn't want to tell Seven, yet. I couldn't eat. The mental exhaustion caught up with me, and I fell asleep on the sofa. I slept the rest of that day and slumbered through Sunday as well.

I woke up at 4:30 Monday morning. I looked a mess and needed a bath. I couldn't wait for the morning paper and logged onto Jacksonville.com to see if there was any info about the accident Saturday.

I searched through the archives to find the article.

WOMAN STRUCK BY CADILLAC

A Duval county man was arrested for vehicular manslaughter in a fatal accident Saturday.

"We feel we have an open and shut case," District Attorney Robert Barclay said. "The driver was tested and high levels of marijuana, cocaine, and alcohol were all found in his system." Witnesses observed the man driving at a speed in excess of 20 mph above the posted speed limit.

"They was flying around that corner," one local resident who spoke on the condition of anonymity said. "Next thing you know... Bam!"

The victim has been identified as Druscilla Thelma Calhoun, 35 years of age, address unknown.

Drugs, drug paraphernalia, and two open alcohol containers were also found at the scene. The name of the driver has been listed as Tripper D. Ought, 18, of 702 New Bold Street. Ought has been out on bond since February 7 awaiting trial on drug-related charges.

Two men where seen fleeing from the scene, one on foot and the other driving a late model red Ford F-150.

CHAPTER TWENTY-TWO

I'm skeptical of banks and their FDIC insurance. I've saved my cash in obscure places since I was winning Earl's lunch money at J. Russell Elementary.

First, I put it in brand-new pairs of long white tube socks, then old Incredible Hulk lunch boxes, now in athletic shoe boxes; all the while bundling stacks and wrapping them in thick rubber bands I collected from the postman.

Rachel still has twenty-something thousand at the hotel. Another four hundred-something thousand sits upstairs on Columbine Drive, plus I have the money Mamasan from the Platinum Kitty Kat gave me at the apartment. My gut is telling me that I can run, but I can't hide and Grandma's Bible taught me that I can't take the money with me when I go.

I called Seven.

"Hello."

"Baby, it's January. Can you come out here and pick me up?"

"I can, but I'm studying for an eight o'clock exam. Can I meet you after class?"

"I tell you what. Meet me at Sister Betty's at 9:30 sharp."

"I can do that. Bye, baby."

"Do well on your test."

"I will."

I dressed in shorts and an Alabama A&M T-shirt and ran around the apartment complex twice, giving me two miles for the day. I did push-ups and jumped rope until my arms and legs quivered, and then took a shower.

Daddy C always said to dress for whatever role you was playing for the day. He looked at the world as a stage and said that we all played a part in the production, either as a puppet or a puppet maker.

I put on a nice Hugo Boss worsted wool two-button charcoal gray suit that I boosted from Daddy C's closet one of those times he was passed out. I selected a light gray cotton Calvin Klein shirt and matching tie, and completed the ensemble with a spit-shined pair of black Kenneth Cole laces-ups.

"Ladies and gentlemen, today's role of 'successful businessman' will be played by January Calhoun, III." I looked in the mirror and laughed.

Calvin the Cabbie put me on Grandma's doorstep at 9:29 A.M., according to my Cartier Pasha wrist wear. The money-green Accord hit the curb at 9:30.

I walked to the front passenger side window. "Good morning, Beautiful."

Seven lowered the window. "Man, you are clean today! What's the occasion?"

"Do you have your briefcase?" I asked.

"I sure do."

"Good. Wait here, and I'll tell you what we're getting ready to do."

Seven took a deep breath and squeezed her hands together.

I unlocked 1326 and bounded upstairs. Grandma is a late sleeper for an older lady. She wakes up at 10:00 A.M. every morning except Sundays.

On Sundays she goes to sunrise service at Pastor Callahan's old church out on US 1 and then to regular morning service at Bethel Baptist downtown. If her schizophrenic neighbor, Auntie Que, is up to it they'll also go worship in the evening with Pastor R. J. Washington on Beach Boulevard.

I made three trips in and out of my old bedroom, placing two shoe boxes in the trunk of the Honda each time–$100,000 per trip.

One of the resident crack heads rode by on his bicycle.

"Hey there, ain't you that Calhoun boy?" he said.

"Good morning, Steamboat. You know it's me."

"Yeah, I thought so. You doing all right?" He rode the bicycle around in a circle while we conversed.

"I'm fine, but I'm busy right now. I have to load some boxes."

"You need some help?" He jumped off the bike, letting it pedal itself until it crashed into Auntie Que's pecan tree.

"Oh, nooo, everything's all right."

"I don't mind. Or does Sister Betty need the yard cut?"

"Yeah, that sounds good. Why don't you come back later and do that?"

He scratched the left side of his forehead for about thirty seconds.

"Let me hold something?"

"I knew that's what this was all about," I said.

"Look, young brother, God knows what He's doing."

"What are you talking about now?"

"I know I ask you for money every time I see you, but, would you rather be me, having to beg people for spare change or would you rather be you, able to give people spare change?" A huge grin came across his face. "It's God's way of evening everything out."

Checkmate. I handed him two twenties and headed back upstairs.

"Thank you, Li'l Calhoun…and good day to you, sister," he said, looking at Seven.

"That grass better be cut when I come back," I said.

Steamboat waved his hand in the air and kept on pedaling.

I left one shoebox in the closet for emergencies. I snuck one box into the kitchen and placed it on an empty shelf in Grandma's spice cabinet, where I was sure she would find it. I left the smallest box, with the least amount of cash in it, in Daddy C's bottom dresser door. It's a little start-up money for when he sees the light of day.

Grandma woke a little earlier than I expected.

"Is that you, January?"

"Hi, Grandma. Bye, Grandma."

"Wait." She stood in her bedroom doorway. "Are you going to the funeral Thursday?"

"No, ma'am. I want to go, but I can't. You have my regards."

"Lord Jesus, I'm only going 'cause she was my daughter." Grandma walked to the top of the staircase and looked down at me standing at the foot of the stairs.

"I understand," I said.

"Boy, if you don't look like your daddy…"

"Who you referring to?"

"Daddy C, who else?"

I wiped my face and rolled my neck.

"She was trying to do right by you, January."

"If you say so, Grandma. I'll never know, right?" I put one hand on the front door.

"Bye, baby." Grandma shook her head. "Take care of yourself."

"Love you, Grandma."

I opened the car door and sat next to Seven. Seeing the anticipation on her face erased the last ten minutes of my life from the foreground of my conscience.

"What's in the shoe boxes?"

"Money."

"Yeah, right. What's in the boxes, baby?"

"Money. Three hundred thousand dollars cash."

"You're serious?"

"Yeah, Seven. Come on, let's go."

Seven pulled away from the curb.

"Where to?"

"First to Wachovia, then Bank of America, then Educational Community Credit Union, then Vystar–any branch will do. We're going to open accounts in your name at each bank."

Seven put one hand in front of her mouth, trying to conceal her smile.

"You'll get Visa check cards for each account. One will be yours to finish school and grad school, and to do as you please."

Seven shook her head in disbelief.

"The rest will be mine. But you keep the cards until I need some cash."

"You trust me like that?"

"Are you telling me something I should know?" I asked.

Seven pulled the Accord to the side of the road and put it in park.

"Get out of the car," she said.

She opened her door and ran to my side of the car. I met her halfway. We hugged and laughed and hugged some more.

"January, I'm yours forever."

I smiled and squeezed her hands.

We spent the rest of the day sampling different types of food, shopping, and going in and out of banks looking like spoiled rich kids converting trust fund money into money market accounts. It was the most fun I've ever had.

Watching Seven smile nonstop for 6 hours, I couldn't help but wonder how long the fun would last.

CHAPTER TWENTY-THREE

Earl Brown had been calling my cell phone for a few weeks, but I hadn't felt like being bothered. Knowing Earl, he was upset about it by now.

I decided to make amends and called him while I straightened the apartment.

"What's up, Earl Brown?"

"Well, well. You finally called somebody back."

I dusted off a picture of our Pop Warner football team. "Quit tripping."

"It's Thursday, ain't it? What, Mike O couldn't squeeze you in for a haircut? You sitting around the house bored?"

"I apologize, B. Come on man…"

"That's what I was waiting on. How you been, black man?"

I sighed. "You heard about my mother, right?" I went into the kitchen to mop the floor.

"Yeah, that's why I was calling, to let you know that I'm praying for you."

Praying for me, I thought. *Not this heathen.*

"Thanks, but what are you talking about, *praying*?"

"I've been trying to tell you for weeks."

"Tell me what?' I rested the mop against my shoulder.

"I got saved, man, baptized and everything. And it's a beautiful feeling."

I resumed mopping. "Is that right?"

"God has delivered me from gambling and drinking and...and He can do the same for you, Boss."

"I don't gamble."

"You know what I mean."

I wrung the dirty water from the mop back into the bucket and carried it down the hall to the toilet.

"Yeah, but you don't think I know that already? I know more Bible verses off the top of my head than you ever knew existed."

"That may be, but there is more to it than that, man." Earl cleared his throat. "You have to allow God to do His will. Acknowledge Him in all thy ways, and He shall direct your path."

"Okay, Brother Earl. You sound like Sister Betty."

"Cool, I won't preach to you, but have Calvin bring you to Kooker Park. We can toss the football, and I'll catch you up on things."

I used Ajax, Soft Scrub, and Pine-Sol to wash down the bathroom.

"Why don't you come and get me?"

"I thought you didn't want anybody to know where you lived."

"You're right. If you don't know, you can't tell."

"My sentiments exactly," he said.

"I'll be there by four-thirty."

"Bet it up."

I finished the bathroom and vacuumed the apartment. I lit incense that I bought from Brother Mike, an intelligent Muslim brother around town who sells anything he can get his hands on.

I ironed my Albany State University baseball jersey and stepped into a pair of Rocawear jeans and gray New Balance and hit the door.

Calvin the Cabbie scooped me up and dropped me by legendary Kooker Park, a professional football player incubator. Seventeen guys who played here back in the day are now in the NFL. Earl and I, and Trip, too, played for them when we were younger. Earl Brown is very much a kid at heart and I found him climbing the monkey bars with some kids.

"What's up, Boss?" He gave me a big hug. "Glad you could make it. I see you still reppin' your Black Colleges." He tugged on my shirt.

"Somebody's got to do it."

He grabbed the football from one of the kids and yelled, "Go long."

"No, you go long." I grabbed the ball from him and he took off. Earl runs a legitimate 4.2 40-yard dash.

I hit him in stride about 60 yards down the field and ran to join him.

"You still got it, huh?" he said.

"You're the one going to play college football for the Rattlers."

"I'm gonna bring them back to the days of Blood, Sweat, and Tears. The coaches at Miami and Florida State couldn't believe I chose FAMU instead of them." Earl laughed.

"You are the first *USA-Today* first team All-American to go there in…uh, um, maybe ever."

"I sure wish you were gonna join me," he said.

I wiped my face and scratched my shoulder.

"Hand me the ball and tell me what's been going on."

"Man, there's so much happening, I'll just tell you the real drama."

We walked to the bleachers, tossing the football back and forth.

"I'm listening," I said.

"First, JSO comes out to that school every other day asking about you. Are you a kingpin or something?"

"Now that's funny," I said.

"No, better yet, are you a ghost or something? Why are they playing like they can't find you?"

"I'm the Invisible Man."

"Yeah, Daddy C really does have some pull, huh?"

"You know the man as well as I do."

"And then too, JSO can't seem to catch that serial killer living behind all those clues, either," Earl said.

"I heard they think it's someone that those girls trusted, but didn't know very well, like a doctor or a mechanic," I added.

Three little girls walked up to us.

"Excuse me, sir, but we have sodas for sale and my mama has some crab cakes in the car."

"Yeah, but I don't drink sodas, sweetheart," Earl said.

"How much are they?" I asked.

The oldest girl scratched her leg. "Well, we have bottled water, also; everything is two dollars."

"Two dollars!" I said.

"Yes, sir. We are raising money to go to cheerleading competition."

"Who is your mama?" Earl asked, and then dropped the football underneath the bleachers.

"The Crab Lady," the youngest sister answered. Earl got up to retrieve the ball.

"Oh, yeah. She can cook, Boss."

"Do y'all have any oranges?" I asked.

"No, sir."

"Okay then. Bring us two cakes apiece and a bottled water for him and one for me."

The two younger girls ran off to fill the order. Earl climbed back up the bleachers with the ball.

I stretched out my legs and rubbed both of my knees.

"That'll be twelve dollars," the remaining sister said.

"Oh, you handle the money, huh?"

"Yes, sir."

The other sisters filled the order faster than most McDonald's.

"Here's twenty dollars. You can keep the whole thing."

"Thank you," they said in unison and ran off waving the $20 bill.

"And y'all better win," Earl hollered.

We dug into the crab cakes. They were tasty. Barking dogs and the thump of eighteen wheel tractor-trailer trucks falling victim to potholes in the road serenaded us until we'd both finished our first cakes. Earl gulped down some water.

"Like I was saying," he started.

"Wait. Excuse me, while I'm thinking about it, I may need two prom tickets," I said.

"Are you serious? I don't think that's a good idea."

"Yeah. Now go ahead with your story."

Earl rubbed the side of his face a few times and wiped at his nose.

"Go ahead, man."

"Well, it's like this… your girl Cindy is out there."

I stopped eating. "What do you mean?"

"She's on it bad. She don't mess with weed no more. That cracker Trip tried to take over the game since you been hiding out. He worked with this dread-headed boy." Earl scratched the back of his head. "He got Cindy on that 'hard.'"

"Crack?"

"Yep. She be over there where Daddy C used to go. What they call it?"

I looked out across the football field. "Hell on Earth."

"She hardly comes to school. Her grades are slipping…"

I thought about how bad she looked last weekend. Why wasn't I able to put two and two together when I saw her?

At the root, this is my fault, I thought.

"I bet she's there right now…not a literal bet–you know what I mean," Earl said.

"Right, but how does she get the money?"

"How do you think she gets the money?"

"Don't tell me that."

"Don't tell you what? Word is *you* gave her a wad of cash."

I stood up.

"I told her to take my money to The Adam's Mark."

"Well, now, I know about that, too, but I couldn't figure it out." Earl stretched his hand out, gesturing for me to be calm. "She did that, but…I heard you gave her permission to keep a li'l bit for herself."

"What's a li'l bit?"

Earl stood to look me in the eye.

"Cuz, she got new Prada bags, Manolo Blahniks, a Rolex watch, and mad clothes. Plus, she feeding her habit."

I stomped to the bottom of the bleachers.

"Come on, man."

"What?" he said.

"Do you still keep your Glock in the car?" I asked.

"Don't even think about it."

"I need your gun and your car. And I need you."

"You can have me and you can have the car, but the gun stays."

"Whatever. I don't need it. I'm a put a foot in somebody's ass. You don't even have to get out of the car, Reverend."

"You gon' bust on Cindy?"

"That's my little sister. I'm a get whoever did this to her."

Earl walked down the bleachers towards me.

"Trip is already locked up."

"Don't worry about all that. Let's go."

Earl and I jogged to his car. Earl put his gun into his empty book bag then put the bag underneath a few boards near the entrance to the park serving as a walkway over the many potholes.

He swung himself into the driver seat and looked into my eyes. I didn't flinch, and he knew not to play with me.

"Let's ride," he said.

CHAPTER TWENTY-FOUR

Hell on Earth isn't exactly the nondescript, unassuming drug haven the addicts who frequent the place would like to believe. If you have *one* of your ears to the street, you'd know about the place. When you're high on drugs, you either think you're being watched by everyone or not seen by anybody.

Earl parked the car three houses down from Hell on Earth. I walked close to the neighboring houses, not out on the sidewalk, and jumped onto the porch of the crack house. I gave the high sign of two fingers placed on my nose and cleared the first security checkpoint. The next one required the five-dollar entrance fee and a quick scan for weapons. Security was light because it was still daylight hours.

These people stayed cocooned in this place working twelve-hour shifts before retiring to the house behind this one, which they also owned, until it was time to clock in again. I suppose they made a boatload of money, but they were so unaware of their surroundings that they didn't recognize me, somebody who grew up right in this general area.

As was expected, it was dark and difficult to see even two-feet in front of me, at first. When my eyes adjusted, I went upstairs. The hardwood floors were in desperate need of refinishing. The banister of the staircase appeared ready to tumble any day now. Black-and-white photographs of different neighborhood legends decorated the walls leading upstairs. There was one of Dr. Mitchell, Daddy C, Dr. H., Steamboat, and myself, among others, all of us suited up and in action on the gridiron or the court. How these pictures were acquired is a mystery to me.

I relieved myself in the upstairs toilet. A five-inch rat lay stuck between the drainage holes in the tub, head down, tail up–an apparent strangulation victim. Dozens of hand towels and several boxes of Irish Spring soap sat on a rack against the third wall.

I looked inside the four bedrooms upstairs and found many walking zombies destroying their lives, but no Cindy. I bounced down the stairs daring anyone in the place to say anything out of the ordinary to me. I was furious.

I headed to the front bedroom downstairs, but heard laughter coming from the back bedroom and changed my course.

Given the environment, there was a nice set of furniture in the front room. The sofas and chairs were a dark color and soft, but full of burns in the fabric. A refrigerator sat in one corner of the room. I found this odd and opened it.

It was full of quarts of Old English and Schlitz Malt Liquor Bull–shit.

"Would you like something to drink?" a voice said.

I turned and faced the 6' 9" bear of a man standing with his arms crossed, hiding the uniform number of his orange Miami Hurricane basketball jersey.

"Naw, nigga," I said and slammed the refrigerator door shut. "Move out my way. I'm looking for somebody."

The laughter grew louder, and I hurried to the back bedroom. Two dirty and wrinkled crack heads blocked the entrance to the door and the view.

"Excuse me. Let me see," I said.

They parted, and I had a front row seat. A light on a small table shone from the front corner of the room, which was no more

than ten feet long by ten feet across. Three men were in this
matchbox of a bedroom. A fat, sloppy-built man wearing his
birthday suit stood in the corner jerking off. A short light-skinned
man stood naked in the middle of the floor with a fistful of $10
crack rocks.

The third man was white–pale to be more precise–and
looked to be in his forties. He stood naked, too, except for a
Florida Marlins baseball cap covering the mop on his head. He had
his penis rammed all the way down Cindy's throat, jerking her
head back and forth with both hands and thrusting his body with
equal force, like he was screwing his pet cat in the back of his
trailer.

He took his penis out of her esophagus, sperm dripping out
of her mouth and onto the floor. The light-skinned man then threw
a few pieces of the crack-cocaine on the floor, and Cindy pounced
on them like a dog fetching a tennis ball. She grabbed the drugs
and scurried to the corner to light up.

"I'm next," the fat boy in the corner said.

"No, I chipped in on the shit. I'm next," the light-skinned
guy said.

One of the fools behind me tapped me on my shoulder.

"All you have to do is buy her a couple of rocks, dog.
She's here all the time."

I turned up my nose at him. "Don't touch me again,
nigga."

"It ain't that serious, Cuz," he said.

"As a matter of fact, I'll tell you a secret." I grabbed him
by his shoulder and whispered in his ear. "By the time I go to that
refrigerator and come back, you probably want to be gone from
here. It's gonna be Aunt Esther in this mug…real ugly."

I could tell he didn't know how to take my warning or was unable to follow directions, one. I approached Six-Nine and asked for two quarts of beer.

"That's ten dollars," he said.

"Do you know me?" I asked.

"Yes, I do."

"Do you know my daddy?"

"Who doesn't?"

"Just checking," I said. I handed him the money and he handed me the brew.

I walked back to the bedroom. Cindy was smoking the crack while the fat boy fondled her breasts.

I approached the man I had warned and shook up the bottles of beer. I set one down and opened the cap on the other and let the contents splash in his face.

"Didn't I tell you to get out of here?" I yelled.

His partner grabbed him by the arm, and they both split.

"What's going on?" the short, light-skinned man asked.

"What do you think it is?" I said. "That's my sister y'all handling like that."

I took both bottles and broke them against the wall. Their faces ballooned with fear. The white boy scatted around gathering his clothes.

"I'm getting out of here," he said.

I waved the broken glass at him.

"Oh, nooo. Especially not you, Jim Crow."

The black men started pleading.

"Cuz, I didn't touch her, never have," one said.

"This is my first time here," the other said.

"Shut up!" I said. "You both sat right there and got turned on by this cracker raping one of your own sisters. I don't want to hear it!"

I set the necks of the bottles I was holding in the corner. The black men picked up their clothes and backed into a corner together.

I approached the light-skinned man and punched him square in the mouth. He dropped his clothes and put up his hands. The white boy stood in the corner and winced.

"Come on and get some," I said to the light-skinned guy.

He threw a wild jab, and I hit him in the stomach and punched him back up against the wall with an uppercut. Jacked up on cocaine and alcohol, what made him think he could hang with me? I guess the cocaine and the alcohol.

His eyes rolled to the back of his head, and he hit the floor. I kicked him in the ribs for good measure. Six-Nine came into the doorway.

"Boss, you can't do it like this."

"Back up Six-Nine. And that's all I'm gon' say."

Six-Nine looked around the room. "Gentlemen, you picked the wrong one."

I rushed to the corner to get my broken beer bottles.

"Cuz, just chill," the fat boy said.

I walked faster towards him. He put up his hands and one of his legs to try to protect his face and body.

"I just want to go home to my wife," he said.

I looked at Cindy. She was passed out; her head lay against the white boy's thigh.

"Your wife, huh?"

"Yeah."

"Does your wife know that you're gay?"

"What are you talking about?"

"Come over here, Jim Crow."

The white boy laid Cindy's body on the floor and came to me.

"Since y'all like oral sex so much–" I looked at the fat boy. "Stick your penis in his mouth."

"You got to be kidding me," the white boy said.

I hit him as hard as I could across the face with the beer bottle. Blood dripped from his ear. The white boy grabbed the side of his head and wiped away some of the blood.

"And let me tell you right now, cracker, if you don't make him come...it's on." I looked back at the black man. "You better enjoy it, you gay-ass nigga."

The white boy slung his hat against the wall, dropped to his knees, and sucked and sucked. I punched him in the side of the face because I didn't think he was working hard enough. I stuck the end of the broken bottle into the brother's behind and tried to spell out CINDY, leaving several small cuts and pieces of glass.

It took no more than five minutes for the black man to start rocking back and forth, enjoying every moment of this disgusting fellatio. The white boy reached up and massaged the fat boy's left testicle, and then he started jerking his own penis.

They came at the same time, and I vomited in the white boy's stringy, sweaty hair.

"You are some sick people," I said.

But I wasn't satisfied. Earl had made his way into the house and back to where we were.

"You all right, Boss?" he asked, as I stabbed the white boy just below his ribs with the jagged edge of the beer bottle.

The man rolled onto his side, unable to pry the glass from his body. I kicked the fat boy in his nuts and punched him twice in the eye when he doubled over to grab his balls.

"Make sure they don't move, Earl."

"Man, what happened?" Earl rubbed his right hand across his heart a few times. "Cuz, you crazy for real."

I picked up Cindy and carried her out. Six-Nine threw a blanket across her naked, unconscious but breathing body, and Earl collected her clothes. I looked Six-Nine in the eye. "Clean this mess up and not a word of this hits the streets."

"That's why they call you Boss."

Earl and I put Cindy in the backseat, bought gas and food to go, and drove straight to Savannah, Georgia. We drank Gatorade and ate steamed shrimp on the way, throwing the shells out of the window like storybook characters leaving a trail back to the house. It wasn't lost on me that my mother was buried that day. There hadn't been a cloud in the sky all week.

Cindy regained consciousness, but slept the entire trip. Earl and I didn't talk much; neither of us knew what to say. I was wrong, and we both knew it.

If I had never messed with drugs, my best friend wouldn't be in this mess, but my story started way before I sold my first ounce of weed...and we both knew that, too.

We took Cindy to Narconon International, a drug rehabilitation center deep in the woods of Georgia, off Skidaway Road, out past Savannah State University. I paid the $10,000 registration fee and signed a promissory note to return with the rest of the money. The rehab center promised to clean up my little sister. Earl Brown promised to never tell a soul.

CHAPTER TWENTY-FIVE

I sat here in this seventy square foot cell, reading and watching different criminals shuttle in and out for the last 56 days, and didn't have a single visitor.

Wait, I forgot. Dr. Mitchell and Dr. H. came to see me about 45 days ago; it slipped my mind. It's an observation; I'm not complaining. I understood that most of my associates couldn't set foot within five hundred feet of this place. The others couldn't be seen conversing with me.

I received a short note from my son two days ago. He said he had a surprise coming for me, but that was it. January never responded in full to my letter. I was concerned about how he was doing. I wondered where he was going to college.

I heard about Dru–oh, well.

"Calhoun!" the C.O. called. "You have a visitor."

I dropped my book, brimming with anticipation.

"You playing with me?"

"I sure am…sit back down." He clapped his hands and laughed.

I should have known better; today is Thursday, not Monday. I retreated to my bunk and continued reading, *Why Should White Guys Have All the Fun* by the late Reginald Lewis, my 23rd book since I'd been detained. I've been riding solo for two days, my longest period of seclusion in years.

"Calhoun!" the C.O. called again ten minutes later. "Make room for your new housemate."

I stood, as I routinely did, to be prepared for any violence my new roommate thought he would use to introduce himself.

"Dr. Lecter meet Hurricane Carter," the C.O. said, cracking himself up. Somebody must have told him he was funny.

"Seriously...Mr. Calhoun this is Mr. de Gucci," he said.

"Of the Gucci Brothers?" I asked.

"That's right, nigga. You ain't know?" de Gucci replied.

The guard glanced at me and closed the door behind de Gucci, who entered the cell, tossed his things on the floor, and began setting rules–in my house.

Get him now or get him later, crisscrossed my brain while he talked.

His arms moved about as he spoke, and I didn't hear a word. My body temperature rose. I opened and closed my hands, flexing my metacarpals. I rolled my neck, causing it to crack and pop. I stood and stretched like a track star or a prizefighter before a championship bout.

I looked into de Gucci's eyes.

"Do you hear me, nigga?" he screamed.

The long lightning bolt-looking scar on his neck was unmistakable. This was the G who tried to kill me!

I blasted that fool with my lucky right hand. *Bam!* He looked stunned and stumbled backwards.

I wasn't taking any chances; there would be no boxing in this fight. I ran to him and struck him across the face with three quick right-handed blows. His nose snapped with the first punch and ran with blood. His left eye swelled and then closed. He hit the floor, knocking his head against the sink on the way down. I wrapped my hands around his neck and face...and pushed his last breath through my fingers and onto the cold floor.

I'll give de Gucci credit; he took his whooping like a man. He didn't cry out one time while I put him to sleep. I quickly lathered a rag and washed his face. I cleaned his neck, thinking that would erase my fingerprints and dressed his bunk.

I laid the recently expired body face first on the mattress. "C.O.!" I called out.

The imitation Bernie Mac came to the cell.

"I think something's wrong with this nigga. He ain't breathing."

"What happened to him?" he asked.

"I don't know." I stepped closer to the C.O. "Nobody wants to be in here. Folk take they own life, every day. I guess they feel guilty for how they was living."

The C.O. straightened his face.

"When will I have my money?" he said.

"My people will take care of you. You just make this go away."

CHAPTER TWENTY-SIX

With no classes to attend, I'd been going to see Mike O for a haircut during the middle of the day. I tried to catch him before lunch, other times after he'd eaten, but whenever I showed up, my open appointment was honored. Oftentimes I fell asleep in the barber chair. If I were awake, I'd put my two cents in one of the Barbershop Forums.

GQ2 is the premier spot for a meticulous professional haircut in Jacksonville. Mike O's two shop mates are good barbers in their own right, but lack the passion that he possesses for his craft, and it shows. The naked eye can't see it, of course, but I pay thirty dollars a week for an hour and a half haircut. I can tell the difference.

The atmosphere of the shop is ethnic and the design Art Deco. Pieces from notable black artists such as Sam Gilliam, Jr.'s abstract talents to ethnic prints by Ernest Crichlow and Kara Walker decorate the shop. You can't go in there and ask, "Saul, why they ain't no brothers on the wall?" like Giancarlo Esposito did in *Do the Right Thing*.

An eclectic mix of music emerges from the Klipsch speakers installed into the walls. Free Dasani bottled water and fresh-squeezed lemonade sit in a large Sub-Zero refrigerator in the back of the shop. Current issues of *Vibe*, *The Source*, and *Essence* magazines sit on the glass coffee table near the front entrance.

Plush oversized chairs in several vibrant colors add flavor to a waiting room setting unheard of in most men's shops in Florida.

Ten female high school students rotate in shifts to wash your hair before a cut and brush you off after one.

Monday through Thursday the staff dresses in matching embroidered or screen printed shirts provided by this mysterious but obviously talented brother around town. No one seems to know his true identity or the location of his shop. He's known simply as T-shirt Man. Friday and Saturday are GQ days. The men wear suits and the females tantalize the patrons in skirts or dresses.

Calvin the Cabbie dropped me off at GQ2 at 1:00 P.M.

It was busy for midday Thursday. I walked by the people in the lobby, pointing my finger at them. I bumped through the traffic to Mike O's chair.

He gave me a pound. "What's up, Mr. Calhoun?"

"How you doing?" I looked around the shop to the other guys seated around the walls. "What's up, black men?"

"I'll be finished in ten minutes, and then you're next." Mike O pointed his clippers around the wall. "You brothers don't mind, do you?"

Everybody motioned that it was cool.

"Take your time. Let me see what these fellas talking about."

"Okay, thanks." Mike O smiled and shook his head; he liked me for some reason. He patted his chest repeatedly and said to the men seated against the wall, "I told y'all we like this."

Four men sat in the chairs out front. One looked my age but wore a Kappa Alpha Psi fraternity windbreaker; I pegged him as twenty-one or twenty-two.

The brother wearing a Howard University homecoming T-shirt said, "I celebrated my thirty-second birthday last Friday, that's how I know."

One brother hinted of forty years of age and kept twisting his wedding band around his finger. The oldest of the group, maybe fifty-five or fifty-six, took off his Masonic baseball cap and rubbed his balding head after everything he said.

I leaned against the wall, flipping through a magazine and listened to get a feel for the conversation before I jumped in.

"I'll be the first to admit it–brothers need it, too," the Masonic brother said.

"Love doesn't just exist in marriages," the thirty-two-year-old said.

"Hell, we know that! That's probably the least likely place to find it," the forty-year-old said.

They laughed.

"But this is what I don't understand," the thirty-two-year-old said. "What's all the fuss about men being players?"

"They called us womanizers, back in the day," the Masonic brother said.

The Kappa brother stood, twirled his cane and did one of their fancy steps. "Players, womanizers, it's all BS," he said. "They act like they are unwilling participants. For us to be players would presume that women are toys; for us to be guilty of womanizing would force the acceptance of a man's natural superiority over a woman and her mind. How else could she be taken advantage of?" He sat and pointed at the other men.

"Now you go back home and you go back to church, and I ask you how many women will instantly disagree with my theory but continue to use those terms as derogatory statements against us?"

"Umm…that's all right, young fella," the forty-year-old said.

"That was more than all right," the fifty-five-year-old said. They laughed again. I sat down next to them.

"How you black men doing? My name is January Calhoun."

The Kappa brother looked at me and squinted.

"You scored 1600 on the SAT. Didn't I read that?"

"Yes, sir, I did, but I don't like to talk about it."

"See, didn't we talk about that last week?" the oldest gentleman asked.

"What's that?" the thirty-two-year-old asked.

"Why is it our young people, our sons in particular, be embarrassed by their accomplishments?" He removed his cap and rubbed his head. "Y'all young niggas so busy trying to show how hard you are, but the younger kids coming up need to see y'all succeed."

"And not just in sports," the forty-year-old said. "I know you, young brother. I know all about you."

You just think you know, went through my mind.

"Shoot, I came through school 'round the same time as your daddy, but up until now, I didn't know you scored no 1600 on the SAT."

"Sir, it's not easy trying to score high on tests, studying, and what-not and maintain my place in the streets," I said.

"Are you talking about street credibility?" the Masonic brother asked.

"Yeah, this is the hip-hop generation," the thirty-two-year-old said, sucking on his teeth. "Street credibility can make you or break you."

"In these times you have to know about Outkast, Zane, Tavis Smiley, Baby and Slim, Cornel West, and T.D. Jakes to be considered knowledgeable. It's a Ghetto Pass, second only to your Player's Card," the Kappa man added.

"The only thing I'm certain about the streets is that if you don't get off them, they'll swallow you up," the forty-year-old said. "You should know that, January."

"What does that mean?" I asked.

"I'm just saying, you should know that."

"You either go to jail, get hooked on drugs, or you get killed." The Mason took off his cap again.

"It's that simple," the thirty-two-year-old said.

Mike O was finished with his client and joined our discussion.

"What are y'all talking about?"

"Ain't nothing much...you ready for me?" I said.

"Yeah, come on."

As I rose to follow Mike O, Theodore de Gucci entered the shop. He is half of the Gucci Brothers who I heard shot up my daddy at the Platinum Kitty Kat.

"I heard y'all could cut up in here. Who wants to take this fifty-dollar bill and tighten me up?"

Darren–one of the other barbers in the shop–snapped a towel in his chair.

"I'll take you right here, Cuz."

Theodore de Gucci plopped his boisterous, obnoxious, gold teeth wearing behind right next to where I was sitting in Mike O's chair. My skin crawled and my hands shook; I wanted to get him.

"Excuse me, Mike O, I need to use the restroom."

"You just went," he said.

"Excuse me, Cuz," I said.

I reclaimed my seat only two minutes later, looking de Gucci in the eye.

"What are you looking at, my nigga?" he said.

"My bad, dog. Don't pay me no attention."

"Naw, I'm the one tripping," he said. "The police picked up my brother last night on some fake-ass charges. They got him shackled downtown right now."

I didn't care anything about that and didn't reply.

I'd washed my hair at home to expedite the process at GQ2. Mike O began the journey.

My head bobbed and weaved, although I knew I needed to stay awake. The hum of the clippers and the tranquility of the shop begged me to fall asleep, and I obliged.

Forty-five minutes passed, and everyone had cleared the shop except for some of the staff, de Gucci, and me. Action Newsbreak interrupted *Oprah*.

With my peripheral vision, I noticed the front door of GQ2 creep open. A large figure dropped and crawled across the floor. All eyes were on the television.

"Bob, what's the situation out there right now?"

"Thanks, Greg. Ah, we are live here at the John E. Goode Pre-Trail Detention Facility. As earlier reported, an inmate has been found dead in his cell. The victim is now confirmed to be twenty-five-year-old Jonathon de Gucci.

"De Gucci had been arrested and convicted on numerous occasions in the past, but had only been in police custody for the past twelve hours before he was found dead in his cell.

"Ah, ironically, Greg, de Gucci was housed in the same cell as January Calhoun, Jr., the father of January Calhoun, III, the honor student and All-American high school basketball star at Durkeeville High School.

"ActionNews has discovered that Calhoun, Jr. was shot six times in an incident at a Beaver Street nightclub in February, that many people believe was perpetrated by de Gucci and his brother,

Theodore. The de Gucci brothers have not been arrested or charged for that crime."

"Bob, has there been any word on a possible suspect?"

"Greg, right now authorities are telling us that it appears to be a suicide."

"Thanks, Bob."

Theodore de Gucci's mouth hung open. He tried to loosen the cape across his body and get up from the barber chair. The person crawling on the floor stood and placed his left hand on de Gucci's chest and waved a .45 in his face.

"What are you gon' do now, Gucci?" he said and tugged on the side of his ski mask.

"Who is that?" de Gucci asked.

A blast went off, hitting de Gucci in the thigh. Darren moved to the opposite side of his chair, out of the line of fire.

"Nigga, what..." de Gucci grabbed his leg. "You shot me."

Two more shots went off, and Mike O grabbed my shoulders.

Two more bullets creased de Gucci's body.

The gunman ran. De Gucci lay in the barber chair with holes in both of his legs, his midsection, and one in his heart.

Watching de Gucci pass away, I pondered if there was some truth about death coming in threes. I wondered if I would make it into Heaven or go straight to Hell. I hope Heaven does have a ghetto.

I needed to holler. I needed to go out back of the shop and scream my stress away, but like so many other times before, I kept my feelings suppressed, bottled and corked by pride.

"Let me finish the back of your head, then I'll call the police," Mike O said.

I stared at the wall ahead of me. "I thought I'd feel better than this," I said.

CHAPTER TWENTY-SEVEN

Seven finished her final exams today and is certain she earned all A's this semester. The first week of May and she is already out for summer break; to me that's one of the biggest benefits of being in college. She wanted to spend some time together to celebrate.

Seven picked me up from the apartment, and we stopped by Regency Mall to return a pair of shoes she claimed didn't fit. Hey, the store clerk refunded her the money. Who am I to question the validity of her claim?

I surprised her with a mini-shopping spree, spending $2,000 on whatever she chose. She selected shoes and more shoes, two nice fragrances, and the beginnings of a new summer wardrobe. I didn't have the final grades in my hand, but her hard work deserved a reward.

Traffic was sparse on the drive back to the apartment. We made a quick stop at Blockbuster. We rented *The Usual Suspects* for the ninth time, *Good Will Hunting*, and the new *Shaft* so that I could trip out on Jefferey Wright's portrayal of Peoples again.

We walked, holding hands, next door to Publix. I purchased two pounds of shrimp, a bag of yellow Spanish rice, and a Vidalia onion. The rest of my secret ingredients were in the kitchen at home.

I prepared Seven a nice Cuban dish Ms. Martinez shared with us at school, and we exchanged massages after eating. She enjoyed her visit to La Casa Calhoun and decided to stay for a few weeks.

"Is that all right with you?" she said.

I needed shower gel and an extra toothbrush to make her feel more at home and readied myself to go back to the store. Seven dictated to me her own lists of wants/needs for the weekend and tossed me the keys to her car.

"I'll be back in a minute," I said.

"Drive safely."

I flipped through Seven's CD case and pushed in the new Outkast offering. I made sure not to rummage the stack of papers she left on the backseat or the collection of envelopes inserted between the sun visor and the roof of the car. I didn't want to find anything that I didn't want to find.

I made it in and out of Publix without incident, buying fifty dollars worth of feminine products, toiletries, and fruit juices. I took the side streets back to the apartment instead of the usual boulevards to break up the monotony.

Big mistake.

I'd forgotten that in the subdivision behind the apartments a burgeoning cocaine trade was taking shape. Being young and black, driving a new car with three thousand dollar rims, I fit the profile for the "random" search at the roadblock I'd driven into.

Twelve JSO officers were out in the streets and walking through folks' yards, escorting narcotics unit K-9 dogs. The afternoon sunlight faded into the west, but still bounced off $250,000 homes and impaired my vision.

"What are you doing in this neighborhood?" the officer asked.

"I'm on my way home."

"You live in one of these mansions?"

I grabbed the steering wheel with both hands and looked straight ahead through the windshield, making sure not to eyeball the officer. "These aren't actually mansions, sir," I said.

The officer pounded his fist on the top of the car.

"Don't get smart with me," he said. "Whose car is this?"

I didn't want to involve Seven in any more mess.

"It's mine," I said.

"What's your name?"

"Boss...Earl Boss."

"Let me see your license and registration, Mr. Boss."

The officer shifted his weight from his left foot to his right, and a rush of sunshine poured into my eyes. I threw my left hand up to block the sun.

"I didn't hear you, officer."

"Requesting backup," he shouted and jerked open the car door.

I had the wherewithal to slam the vehicle into park just as the cop released my seat belt and snatched me from the car.

He was cock strong for his size and had no problem body-slamming me to the pavement.

Other officers ran towards us. "Freeze" and "Don't move!" stood out as the commotion ensued. One officer jammed his knee into my spine.

"He's got a gun," the initial JSO flunky lied.

Another officer punched me in the face, but it didn't hurt. I looked in his direction to read his badge and spit on his shoes. I mentally scribbled Officer Maiden on my list.

K-9 dogs were brought in to sniff the car. Rich white people came outside in swimsuits and untied house robes, cheering on the JSO efforts. Officers searched in and around the Honda Accord for the imaginary firearm.

"Someone call in this name: Boss. Earl Boss."

The officers lifted me up and forced me against the car.

One of them searched my pockets and found $2,500 in fifty-dollar bills. Upon their discovery, handcuffs were slapped on my wrists so tight that they pinched me. It hurt, as did the knee to the back and the body slam, but I refused to let them white boys see me cry.

The name Earl Boss came back clean and the lead harassment official made me an offer I couldn't refuse.

"Son, this is a lot of money for someone your age to be carrying around."

I looked at him, knowing where he was going with this and wanting to pull the hairs out of his head one by one.

"We can take you down to the station and make you tell us where you got it and what you were about to do with it in *this* neighborhood."

"Or?" I asked.

"Or you can go. The money stays," he said.

"Take these cuffs off me." I rolled my neck, causing it to crack and pop.

"Do we have a deal?"

"Yeah, man. Get these things off me."

The officer unlocked the shackles and placed them on his holster. He grabbed both sides of my face and kissed me on the cheek.

"Thank you, pretty boy," he said.

He fanned the money in the air and yelled out, "Boys, strip club tonight, yeah!"

The group of them whooped and hollered like the redneck trailer park trash they are in their hearts.

I drove off, leaving the dirty dozen in my rearview mirror– not a good cop amongst them.

CHAPTER TWENTY-EIGHT

During the entire two weeks Seven stayed with me at La Casa Calhoun, I didn't mention the incident behind the apartments. She asked about the scratch on my chin, but I dismissed it as a self-inflicted wound.

She needed to go on campus to discuss the possibility of attending summer school with her academic advisor. *We* needed to go today because being out in public was the surest way to keep our hands off each other. Our loins needed a break.

We drove I-95 with the windows down, a/c blowing, and vintage 2 Live Crew bass pounding our chests. Uncle Luke raised our parents and their lessons became our lessons.

We exited the interstate at Kings Road and passed the main branch of the U.S. Postal Service, still traveling at highway speeds. As we neared Myrtle Avenue, I asked Seven to slow down.

"Let's stop by and see Sister Betty real quick."

She made a hard right turn without breaking stride. (The jury is still out on the possible revocation of licenses for women drivers).

Seven pulled next to the curb in front of 1326, thirty seconds later. Auntie Que was out watering her lawn and Steamboat was trimming Grandma's hedges.

"Hello, Auntie Que," I said.

She waved at me as if she were fanning a gnat.

"The yard look good, don't it?" Steamboat said with a big smile on his face.

I gave him three dollars before he could ask.

"Thank you, Li'l Calhoun," he said. "Look here, why don't you let me paint the house for you. Five hundred dollars will do it."

"Five hundred dollars…" I said. "Go 'head on, Steamboat. I ain't got time for that."

Seven tugged on my hand, and we climbed the stairs to the porch. I unlocked the front door and found Grandma in the kitchen.

"Is that you, January?"

"Yes, ma'am."

She was cooking up a storm. She wore the apron I made her in the third grade with my tiny handprints emblazoned around the slogan MY GRANDMA IS THE BEST…HANDS DOWN.

She gave me a big hug.

"Grandma, this is my girlfriend, Seven Tennille," I said. "Seven, this is my grandmother, Sister Betty."

"Nice to meet you, young lady." Grandma squinted. "Are you two in the same class together?"

"No, ma'am. I'm a student at Edward Waters College."

"I thought you looked a li'l older than my baby." Grandma hit me on the arm with her kitchen towel. "She's a beautiful girl, though.

"Is my grandson treating you right?"

"Yes, ma'am, I don't know what I'd do without him." Seven grabbed my right arm with both hands and kissed my cheek.

"Don't be like his mama and mess up a good thing spreadin' yourself around the neighborhood."

Seven shifted her eyes from side to side, not wanting to touch that subject.

"Grandma, what are you doing in here? There's enough food for all of Columbine Drive."

"Head Start is having their end-of-the-year cookout and I volunteered to fix a few of my specialties."

I looked on the counters in the kitchen. There were more than "a few" items.

"I started last night. I'll be finished in five more minutes. Look in the fridge," she said. "I fried twenty-two pounds of fresh chicken wings, cleaned and cooked four bunches of collard greens. Let's see…I fixed two casseroles of macaroni and cheese. I seasoned seventy-three dollars' worth of fish that we'll fry when I get there and baked three cakes and one sweet potato pie."

"Sweet potato pie?" I said.

"That's for you. I knew you'd be coming by sooner or later," she said. "If it was later, I would have froze it 'til you came.

"But you came sooner…and right on time to help me take everything to Head Start, since we can't call on Calvin the Cabbie no more."

"Why not? What happened?" I asked.

"You didn't see the paper this morning? It's in there on the table. Go look at it, the front page."

My regular cabdriver made the front-page headlines! It was reported that he was the mysterious serial killer terrorizing our city. According to the paper, he strangled five people, all women, all black, and all passengers in his taxi. Damn!

"Seven, come read this. You're not going to believe it."

I handed her the newspaper and went to the downstairs bathroom. I relieved myself and passed Seven returning to the kitchen. I rubbed her shoulder.

"You all right?" I said.

"Yeah. This is incredible," she said, pointing at the newspaper.

I pushed open the swinging door to the kitchen and noticed that I didn't hear any pot or pan tops clanging or any timers going off. Grandma hummed one of several old Negro spirituals whenever she thought she had put her foot in a dish. I didn't hear any humming, either.

A thick trail of Lawry's seasoned salt began at the foot of the stove and led to Grandma's body stretched out on the floor.

I checked her pulse. I took a deep breath to calm myself and checked it again because I didn't feel one the first time.

I felt a slow thump…thump the second time. I searched through her spice rack, where she thought no one knew that she hid her blood pressure medicine, and found the full medicine bottle.

"Why won't she take care of herself?" I mumbled.

"Seven, come quick, please."

Seven pushed open the door to the kitchen.

"Oh, my God…what's wrong?"

I tossed the bottle of pills into the air and Seven caught them.

"She hasn't been taking her medicine. She's probably overexerted herself with all this cooking."

"I'll call an ambulance."

"We don't have time. Let's take her in your car."

Seven and I lifted Grandma from the floor.

"Hold on," Seven said.

She turned off the eyes on the stove and made sure the oven was off. She locked the windows in the kitchen and the front room while I held Grandma against my shoulder.

When Seven was satisfied that the house was secure, we carried Grandma to the car and put her in the backseat.

I called ahead to Jasmine at University Hospital.

"Who are you calling?" Seven asked.

"A nurse at the hospital," I said.

Nurse Jasmine, a doctor, and one of the big portable hospital beds awaited us. They rushed Grandma through the double doors and took her wherever you take people who suffer from high-blood pressure and refuse to treat it.

"Everything will be all right," Jasmine said. I hugged Seven and asked her to take the food to Head Start.

One of the reasons was so that Grandma's efforts wouldn't be in vain and the other was to prevent Seven from getting a good look at Jasmine.

"Here are the keys to the house. If Steamboat is around have him help you, but don't give him a dime. Tell him I'll pay him later."

"Okay, but where is Head Start?"

"Take Myrtle Avenue south until it dead ends into Forest, and turn right. Forest Park Head Start is a quarter mile down on the right."

Seven walked away, and then returned.

"Who do I need to see?"

"Look for another volunteer by the name of Ms. Patrick. She's a plus size woman with a heart and personality to match her size," I said. "Everybody knows her, but if you can't find her...I don't really know. They all are good people– from the nutrition staff to the bus drivers to all the teachers."

"So anybody will do?"

"It ain't gonna be nothing. I used to go through there a li'l bit. If they know you're with me or Sister Betty, they'll take care of you."

"Okay. Myrtle Avenue, Forest, Ms. Patrick," she said.

"You got it."

"I'll call you on my way back here."

"Thanks, baby. I'll be all right," I said.

Seven exited the emergency room doors as Jasmine entered the waiting room from the other side.

"Mr. Calhoun, may I speak to you?"

The police officer on duty drank from his Coca-Cola bottle, and then tipped his cap to me. I looked away.

"Mr. Calhoun?" Jasmine said again.

I stood and walked to her.

"Your grandmother would like to speak to you."

"Is she going to be all right?"

Jasmine walked five feet ahead of me and didn't answer. We rounded the fourth corner of the maze and Jasmine pointed. "She's in there."

A tangled mess of intravenous infusion ran from different apparatus into different parts of my grandmother's body. The blinds were unopened and only a small fluorescent light glowing above her head provided any light.

She turned to me as I neared her bedside.

"Thank God you're alive."

Grandma managed a weak smile.

"Why do you do this to me?"

"Son, I want to be with my Lord."

Grandma moaned and rolled her head. She reached for my hand and squeezed tightly.

"January, my days are numbered, and I need to tell you some things."

"I don't want to hear that kind of talk, Grandma," I said.

"You're almost a man now. I'm gonna go 'head and let loose of what's really killing me," she said. "Pull that chair up and sit down."

I did as told and grabbed her hand again.

"Son, your mama loved you, but she wasn't no good. Your daddy was drinking when they met, sure enough, but she the one got him hooked on those drugs."

"What do you mean?"

"January Calhoun, Jr., was the sweetest man to walk the streets of Durkeeville 'til another January Calhoun came along and took his place." She let go of my hand and wiped under her eye.

"He was the hero of the community, a big, big star in the city of Jacksonville."

I scratched my shoulder.

"His parents died three days before Christmas when he was 12 years old; some Christmas present, huh? He raised himself from there."

The light over her head flickered a bit then regained its full glow.

"They left him a whole bunch of money–in coffee cans. He still got some, don't let him fool you."

I raised my eyebrows.

"He made what was left of the money grow in the stock market when you were still at J. Russell. How you think he affords all those expensive suits? He only wants to spend his money on clothes. He wanna beg people for money for his habits. See, in his heart he knows it's not a good use of money."

"Makes sense," I said.

"How many drug addicts do you know dress up every day for 'work'. Your daddy's not stupid; he's a very smart man. Ask him, he'll tell you." Grandma laughed, and the pain of laughter almost brought her to tears.

"He just weak." She grabbed my hand again. "That comes from that heart of his. January gave money to every politician in this city, all the top people in the state. He gave money to Head

Start, the Police Athletic League, and in general, to anybody who asked."

"He had it like that?" I said.

"There were people who made millions in stocks and bonds in the 90's."

"It's hard to imagine."

"Your daddy is connected! You're talking about a football hero, a basketball star who's smart and has more friends than the law allows. Do you know how powerful that combination is in this country?"

I didn't.

"He just had to have your mama. She was the finest thing in town. But she was always out for self. I don't know why or what I did wrong, but she started in on the drugs and did your daddy like Eve did Adam."

I ran my hand across my hair.

"But out of all that, this is what you need to know." I sat back in the chair. "Your daddy is your daddy."

"What are you saying, Grandma?"

"I guess you've never looked in a mirror. January Calhoun, Jr., is your father, your biological father."

"But I thought..." I said.

"Druscilla was half crazy. God gave her a body, but very little common sense." Grandma took a deep breath and exhaled. "She wanted out of her marriage, wanted out of Durkeeville. Said she was going to Hollywood to be a movie star; you don't want to know what kind of movies she ended up making."

"But she didn't leave until I was nine years old. I remember that."

"Daddy C tried to make it work. He tried for five years after she told him that lie about you not being his. Seems like the more he tried, the more she rejected, the more drugs he abused."

I nodded like I understood, but my emotions were getting the best of me.

"He grew up alone. He wanted to be loved like anybody else. He wanted somebody to need him. When Dru left, he tried to transfer that love to you, but he never could get it right."

My head was buried in my hands; misty eyes cleared a pathway for a flood of tears. I stood and stuck my head deep into Grandma's chest. She rubbed my head, back and forth, trying to ease the pain.

It's hard being a child trapped in a man's world.

CHAPTER TWENTY-NINE   *May 27ᵗʰ*

Dear Chevy,

    The walls are closing in on me. The Trinity of Death stopped by for a visit. My mother's gone forever, for sure now. My father is locked up. My grandmother is laid up in a hospital. My best friend is in a rehab center, and there are a host of other problems.

    My two bright spots are you and Seven. You've been faithful for years; you I can count on, but how long can I hide the real me from my girl? Will she love me in spite of my faults? Depends on the faults, huh? Then I guess I can kiss her good-bye.

    My size and my reputation have people fooled. I am not a robot. Red blood flows through my veins like all living creatures. I have feelings, and I need love, too. I believe in God like the rest of this nation that is under Him. I am proud to be associated with Queen Nzinga and Marcus Garvey, but don't want to live any other place on Earth. I am intelligent and yet, unknowing. I have read, but continue to read. I am lost, but want to be found.

                             Love,
                             January III

CHAPTER THIRTY

"Dr. Mitchell, this is January Calhoun, III."

"Damn, son, where are you?"

"I'm at home, but no time for that. I need a favor."

"Don't you think your favors have run dry?"

"Listen. I'm still the valedictorian, right?"

"That depends. If we don't count this semester, you might still have a chance, but–"

"Withdraw me from this semester and I can keep my average. I want to speak at graduation."

"Son, do you know what we are facing right now?"

"Yeah, ten to twenty, but I don't care about that. I need to free my soul."

Dr. Mitchell didn't respond.

"Dr. Mitchell?"

"I'm here."

"Please let me do this." I took a deep breath and exhaled. "Nothing lasts forever. It's the chance you take to live how you want to live, to do what you want to do."

Dr. Mitchell breathed heavily into the phone, but didn't speak.

"Do I have to call Dr. H.?" I said.

"Boy, I don't care if you call Daddy C. I'm the principal–I run this here!"

"Calm down, sir."

"I don't like what you're trying to pull!"

"You know as well as I do who runs what around where. May I *please* speak at graduation?"

"Okay, Mr. Smart Man. 'Boss'. Do your thing. Go ahead and make your farewell speech, but understand this: I am not going down with you."

"Dr. Mitchell, you know I'm not a rat, but this here is deeper than a letter society. Your Omega brothers can't help you now."

Dr. Mitchell slammed the phone down in my ear. I looked at the phone I held in my right hand. "He's got a lot of nerve," I mumbled.

I rose from the dining room table and set my empty Kool-Aid glass in the kitchen sink. I retreated to the living room, grabbed the remote control and changed the program to *SportsCenter*.

I threw my tired body onto the sofa and watched a parade of clips depicting professional basketball players missing shot after shot, hoisting brick after brick. I couldn't hear the commentary, but the visual made it seem as if today's players couldn't throw the ball in the ocean if they had to.

Next thing I know, they are replaying taped footage of Trip D. Ought, my old friend, with his hands and feet shackled walking with several prison officials and hordes of television reporters and cameramen accompanying them. In the top right hand corner of the TV is a picture of me!

I increased the volume on the set. They cut to Trip seated at a red cloth-draped tabled behind seven or eight microphones.

He looked at a piece of paper and solemnly read. "My name is Trip Ought and I am of no significance to society at this stage of my life except for the fact that I possess discriminating evidence against some of the most important and recognizable people in the state of Florida and thus, this country at large.

"I have entered into a plea bargain with the State Attorney's Office and the prosecuting attorney concerning an earlier drug possession with intent to sell charge and my recent case in the accidental death of Ms. Druscilla Thelma Calhoun, mother of USA-Today All-American basketball player January Calhoun, III. My charges in both cases have been reduced in exchange for testimony against January Calhoun, III and his well disguised drug trafficking empire."

He can't be doing this, I thought. Camera bulbs flashed at amazing speeds. Chairs screeched across the floor, papers shuffled. Trip straightened himself in the chair and continued.

"January Calhoun, III known as Boss on the streets of Durkeeville, Florida, and the surrounding area of Jacksonville, possesses one of the most intricate, complex, sophisticated, and sinister minds of any seventeen-year-old in America. I know this because I was once part of his clandestine operation. From my own savings, I can reasonably guestimate January Calhoun, III's personal fortune to be in the five million to six million dollar range.

"January has a particular fascination for orange–the fruit and the color. He and his gang have adopted the color and the fruit as their signature mark and sign by which one may know another in the dark as well as in the light.

"Boss's network includes his own crack-cocaine addicted but well-connected father, January Calhoun, Jr., legendary high school basketball coach and current Durkeeville High School principal Dr. Juan Mitchell, and the current boys' basketball head coach of the same high school Dr. Leroy (Dr. H.) Herman Hawk–the single largest black property owner in Duval County. His group also includes state politicians, local police, local postal workers, ruthless underground figures, and others, some of whom are unsuspecting and have fallen victim to January Calhoun's extreme generosity, charisma, and lethal intellectual aptitude–even when unarmed January Calhoun should be considered dangerous."

Trip finally let out the carafe of tears he'd sniffled and coughed back into their ducts the entire press conference. The drops crawled down his face like raindrops on faceted glass at a small country church.

Trip then stared straight into my eyes as the cameraman pushed in for a close-up.

His message was for me. "Do as I say, not–"

I pressed down hard on the power button of the remote control. I didn't want to hear another word.

CHAPTER THIRTY-ONE

It was a bright lukewarm Friday June 6, thirteen days before the big Juneteenth celebration and twenty-eight days before my eighteenth birthday. After *The Trip D. Ought Show*, I needed a quiet place to brainstorm a game plan. Rachel allowed me to sequester myself in a 12th floor suite, but the game plan never came.

I'd been here at The Adam's Mark Hotel for the last week. Different sets of 10-digit codes had been blowing up my cell phone but going unanswered without proper identification.

I switched my focus to my commencement address. I was no longer concerned about my immediate future; it was apparent that I'd secured that with my immediate past.

Seven spent the last two nights with me. Last night we talked and kissed for hours. I kissed her everywhere, until the hairs rose off her back and her toes curled into bows of satisfaction.

"January, are you finished with your breakfast?" she asked. "If you are, hurry up and get ready, baby."

Seven selected and purchased an amazing cream-colored FUBU suit and a pair of teakwood brown lace-up Johnston & Murphy shoes to match for me. The shirt, tie, and pants were ironed and spread across the bed.

Seven was already dressed in a similar ensemble accented by a bead of pearls that made her look both several years older and the perfect accompaniment.

After a quick shower, I dressed, and Seven and I strolled arm-in-arm to the house limousine Brad arranged to deliver us to the Times-Union Center a few blocks away where commencement exercises where being held for three other high schools as well as for Durkeeville High.

The driver parked in front of the building, and we waited inside. Several of my classmates approached the vehicle and attempted to peer through the dark tinted windows. No one had any idea I was inside.

My cell phone rang. The caller ID displayed Dr. Mitchell's cellular number.

"Good morning," I answered.

""January, it's Dr. Mitchell. Are you in the white limousine parked out front?"

"Why?"

"I figured as much," he said. "This is my last favor for you. Have the driver pull up about forty yards. I'll jump in and take you to the back entrance of the theatre."

"Driver, pull ahead please," I said. "Slowly, please."

I saw Dr. Mitchell standing between two uniformed JSO officers, all three partially obscured by a large bush. When we'd driven the forty yards, Dr. Mitchell stepped to the curb, away from the officers, holding an awkward-sized package. They turned their backs and surveyed the area.

"Stop here and let this man in, please."

The driver did, and Dr. Mitchell entered the rear of the limo with us.

He signaled to the driver. "Take three quick rights, and we'll enter from the food service entrance."

He turned back to face us. "Good morning, Ms. Seven. You look very nice today."

She waved. "Thanks."

Dr. Mitchell nodded. "Mr. Calhoun."

"Hello, sir. Thanks for everything."

I looked out of the window. "Trip was your choice, you know?" I said.

Dr. Mitchell shrugged. "I know. I made a mistake. What can I do?"

I reached out, and Dr. Mitchell met me halfway. We held each other for what seemed like ten minutes.

"We agreed you would take the fall," he said.

"I'm the one who set the game in motion. I haven't forgotten," I said.

"No one knows you're here, but JSO provides security for these affairs. There is an APB out on you..."

"Will I be able to finish my speech?"

Dr. Mitchell handed me the package he was holding. "It's your cap and gown. Put it on." He smiled. "I've never known you to be afraid, son."

"I'm not a quitter; I just have some things I need to say."

"If they do get you today, before your birthday and all, we're good to go," he said.

"I thought about that."

Dr. Mitchell looked at his Rolex. "It's time. Everyone should be seated. You will sit behind the other distinguished guests, and I will introduce you." Dr. Mitchell shook my hand. "You're on your own after that."

CHAPTER THIRTY-TWO

From there, everything became a bit dreamy, delightful, but less precise. The applause was louder than I expected. Excluding Seven's adoration, I hadn't felt this much love since the championship in early March, 90 days to a calendar, but more than 129,000 minutes to my heart.

It dawned on me that this was what I needed. It was what we all needed. Moved by the reception, I opened my speech differently than I had planned.

My smile stretched across the stage, and I opened my arms wide to match. "*All we need is a little love,*" I said.

My classmates and their friends and family in the audience stood and cheered again, this time louder than before. Seven simple words birthed pandemonium in the Times-Union Center.

"Thank you, everyone. Thank you." I nodded and motioned for the crowd to take their seats.

"This little bit that I want to share with you this morning is for no one in this place in particular and for everyone in the building in general." I looked around the auditorium. "The Bible says that there are times when all men cannot receive what is being said, only those for who it is purposed shall receive it. I pray that all who can understand what I am talking about today…will understand it."

I looked over my shoulder and checked for JSO. "My concern is with parents and parenting."

"Yeah, tell 'em," someone in the crowd yelled.

"Why are parents afraid of their children? How are little girls divorcing their parents? Why are there so few Chiefs to manage so many Indians? You might think that it matters not how other children are raised or if they are trained at all, but it does. It will matter when the same boy that you chose not to help with his homework or catch passes with, grows up to rob your grandmother or sexually assault your sister. It will matter a lot then, won't it?"

"It sure will," Dr. Mitchell offered behind me.

"Adults, I beg you to start encouraging us. Motivate us to want to be more than a professional football player. Help us to explore all our different talents." I removed a handkerchief from my back pocket and wiped my mouth. "When I was twelve years old, I told my grandmother, Sister Betty, that I wanted to be a writer when I grew up. You know what she said to me? She said, 'Write what?' "

"No she didn't," came from my right.

"I was floored. I didn't have an exact answer; I only knew that I wanted to put words on paper. It was her job to open my eyes to the different possibilities."

I paused and looked to see if I had the crowd's undivided attention and it appeared I did.

"I wanted to speak up for myself but my esteem was unequal to today's
back then I had skinny legs, no chest, and doo-rags covered my waves.
Folks around me talked about 'good' hair, smaller noses, and less melanin,

I didn't know for a long time it's a beautiful skin that I'm in.

I did find self-worth, but in the wrong places—I found it in the streets

I found it in ill-gotten dead presidents; I found it under pink satin sheets.

I learned to dribble a ball low and jump with it or to get it, very high

Daddy C slurred that I needed to add, needed to read, and that I needed to write.

I came up with a praying grandma and a man who claimed me, but I was alone

then I met a friend girl and we washed dishes while we talked on the phone.

I promptly led her down the wrong path, and I followed closely behind

a classic case of the blind leading the blind, leading the blind.

No other race on Earth goes thru what we go thru to do the little that we do

latch-key our kids to get a second job, then ignore groceries to buy new shoes.

I might not speak; I refuse to shake your hand, definitely not giving you a hug

but we have the same color skin, the same big butts, and the same high blood

Pressure to floss like our neighbor leads us to weeds, and to rocks, to make gains,

but Judge White treats Mr. Black like a piece of crack is the same, as a kilo of cocaine.

So another one of us gets a personal escort downtown or to Jesup, GA last count was over two million inmates, but that number grabs every day.

The few men left around spread thin or talk trash because we can,

our sisters are educated and beautiful, but don't have their own man

and the same can be said for our sons and our daughters– two of God's gifts,

the audacity to reject Him on those and still beg for the rest of our wish lists.

I'm just talking to y'all today, issues been on my mind since I was a child

if you gon' have the child, raise the child, and you have to do it the whole while.

There are no time-outs, no off-seasons, no trades, no instant replays,

your job is like a year of our Lord, it lasts three hundred sixty five days.

Bad parents breed bad children–take it from me, I'm Durkeeville All-Madden

being the best of the worst, for my life, is not what I imagined.

Look at me today, look at my girl, and look at Daddy C when he's dressed up

I've decided right now, just because my parents are, I don't have to be messed up.

It all starts with a dream, a dream to do better,

close your eyes with me and release all that wouldn't let ya

Move forward and improve and claim a new place in this life,

it's the only one you're going to get, at least die trying to live it right."

I backed away from the podium and took a bow. Cheers and rhythmic clapping filled the auditorium. I heard screaming, cheering, and then, loudest of all, tearful moans and a chorus of boos. I remained calm, as I was taught to do in all endeavors, determined to make a better life for myself, as if the harder I thought about it the greater the possibility of it happening today, right now.

My ego told me that I was the leader of this pack, but what's upsetting about that? Curiosity spoiled my concentration, and I looked across my right shoulder.

There they were; parallel to me, about ten yards to the right of the podium. Seven or eight JSO officers approached me with handcuffs open and guns drawn.

I stuck out my hand like a human stop sign. "Can I speak to my girl before we go?"

"You have two minutes," the lead officer said.

I motioned for Seven to come quick.

I whispered in her ear. "Go to Old Pappy Johnson's front yard–I mean back yard–and find the '68 Chevy Impala."

Seven grabbed me close and hugged me tight.

"Listen, baby, hit the license plate real hard, kick it if you have to." I glanced at the officers. "The trunk will open–" I leaned closer to her ear–"and you will find another two million reasons to wait on me 'til I get out."

I grabbed her face with both of my hands and kissed her forehead. Seven started to cry. "Baby, I'm only seventeen years old. What can they do?"

She hugged me again. I pried myself from her grip and returned to face the officers.

The first cop stepped to me and slapped the warrant for my arrest in my palm. My classmates yelled and cursed the officers.

They flung their caps onto the stage. People from the audience threw whatever they could find–lipstick, quarters, miniature liquor bottles, and chicken leg bones...

The crowd was so loud that I could barely hear the officer call my name.

"Jan- u –ry Cal-n. You-der-est for..." his mouth moved, but I couldn't hear him. "You...the right...silent..."

Since I did, and since I was tired, and since I knew I was dead wrong, the rest of the righteous man's words fell upon weary and defeated ears.

CHAPTER THIRTY-THREE

I appreciated Dr. Mitchell extending me the opportunity to address my classmates as the official valedictorian at graduation.

I had become the second person in my family to earn that honor. Most families never have one person related to them ranked first in their high school class, let alone two.

I believe what I wrote was appropriate and necessary for that particular audience. The words came from my heart and from the minds of my generation from Oakland to Atlanta, from Miami to Flint, Michigan.

It's a shame that a speech so important, so passionately written and lyrical in verse had to go to waste. It's a tragedy that no one got to hear it.

Seven and I never made it through the food service entrance to the auditorium.

We exited the limo and jogged towards the doorway. I'd decided to put on my cap and gown in the auditorium bathroom; we looked too good in our suits. Professional photographers hired to immortalize the graduation ceremony and members of the press lined our path.

"There he is," someone shouted.

Bulbs flashed with each photograph. Squirrels raced through dried grass, darting back and forth, undecided which way to go. The sun shone directly on us like a theatre spotlight.

"Hold on to me." I pulled Seven closer. "Why are all these people here?"

A familiar face approached me. Though the upper torso and lower body were draped in a navy blue suit, I would have known those piercing blue eyes and thick dark eyebrows anywhere.

Officer Maiden, the cop who beat me out of $2,500 dollars, rushed to my mind, and my temper got the best of me for the last time.

He held up his badge. "January Calhoun, you are under–"

I pushed Seven to the ground and punched the officer in the mouth two times while I held his coat jacket with my other hand.

"January, don't," Seven cried out then crawled away from danger.

Two of Officer Maiden's teeth flew from his mouth. I grabbed him by his shoulders and sent a knee crashing through his nose. I felt the sensation of his nose breaking from my leg on into my stomach. The blood from his face threatened to ruin my suit. Orlando Maiden flopped over backwards like a domino.

And I did, too.

The remaining undercover JSO officers opened fire on me and riddled my lungs and pancreas with seven bullets. The food service trucks parked around me took more of a pounding than I did, but I was through for the day, just the same.

I dreamed of presenting my speech to the class from a hospital bed during the most peaceful sleep I'd had in the last three years.

In a coma for 38 hours, I reminisced about my life from start to present. I visited Orlando where I was born; traveled to J. Russell Elementary where I met Earl, Trip, Cindy, and the Chevy Impala; and knelt down at Bethel Baptist Institutional Church were

I learned Romans 8:38-39. I stopped by the Platinum Kitty Kat where Dr. H., Dr. Mitchell, Mamasan, Daddy C, and I pledged our allegiance and outlined our assignments, and I dribbled to Durkeeville High where I rose high and fell hard in a very short time.

I awoke from the coma to the sounds of my own voice reciting the 23rd Psalm. Sister Betty and Seven flanked my bed, each holding one of my hands, praying and loving me back to life.

The JSO officer stationed at my door, periodically looking in on me and the web of intravenous infusion shackled to my body would prove to foreshadow Daddy C's and my own fate for the next 18 months, but at least I was alive and ready to be rehabilitated.

You can learn something from anybody, including the most unlikely candidates. Daddy C is a drug addict and has been wrong most of the time, most of my life. And it is true that the best leaders lead by example. But Daddy C isn't a leader anymore. He's just a man who wanted better for his son.

He'd already told me everything I needed to know in one short sentence. I should have listened.

To order copies, please send money order
or institutional checks to:

Written In Black Publishing

P.O. Box 9303

Jacksonville, Fl 32208

Please include: Name

Address

E-mail (if any)

and $13.95 + $3.95 shipping.

(Only $2.00 shipping for each addt'l book.)

www.frederickpreston.com

Credit card orders please visit website